DATE			

THE ABDUCTORS

CONSPIRACY

THE ABDUCTORS

CONSPIRACY

JONATHAN FRAKES

WITH

Dean Wesley Smith

A TOM DOHERTY ASSOCIATES BOOK
TOR® NEW YORK

This is a work of fiction. All the characters and events portrayed in this novel are either fictitious or are used fictitiously.

THE ABDUCTORS: CONSPIRACY

This book is printed on acid-free paper.

A Tor Book
Published by Tom Doherty Associates, Inc.
175 Fifth Avenue
New York, NY 10010

Tor Books on the World Wide Web:
http://www.tor.com

Tor® is a registered trademark of Tom Doherty Associates, Inc.

Design by Fritz Metsch

Library of Congress Cataloging-in-Publication Data

Frakes, Jonathan.
The abductors : conspiracy / Jonathan Frakes and Dean Wesley Smith.
p. cm.
"A Tom Doherty Associates book."
ISBN 0-312-86208-3
I. Title. II. Smith, Dean Wesley.
PS3556.R26A64 1996
813'.54—dc20 96-23846
CIP

First Edition: December 1996

Printed in the United States of America

0 9 8 7 6 5 4 3 2 1

To the invaluable Lisa J. Olin, without whom none of this would have happened.

THE ABDUCTORS

CONSPIRACY

Prologue

When fate's got it in for you there's no limit to what you may have to put up with.

—GEORGETTE HEYER
FROM *A BLUNT INSTRUMENT*

JUNE 18.
SALMON RIVER PRIMITIVE AREA

The campfire crackled, sending golden sparks drifting up a few feet into the air before they went black and disappeared as if they had never existed. For a moment the small fire seemed calm. Then a log moved, the fire crackled, and golden sparks again drifted upward and vanished.

A thousand feet overhead, far higher than the smoke from the fire would ever reach, the last of the sunset tinted the tops of the high mountain ridges with a faint red. Above the ridges a few stars fought and won against the last of the day. It was a battle that was fought every night, over and over.

The stars always won.

Nineteen-year-old Jerry Rodale leaned back, his head

resting on his rolled-up sleeping bag as he stared up through the tall pine trees at the emerging constellations. He pulled his light jacket tight around his chest and stuffed his hands into his jeans pockets. It would be a clear, crisp night in the Idaho mountains. A beautiful night for stargazing.

Around him the dull roar of water rushing over rocks filled the steep-walled mountain valley. The Middle Fork of the Salmon River started twenty miles above this point and ninety miles away ended in the main Salmon River, flowing into the "River of No Return" canyon. Eventually the water passing by now would reach the Pacific Ocean near the beautiful city of Portland, Oregon. But in this valley tonight, fifty miles from the nearest town and twenty miles from the nearest road, there were no sounds of civilization. Only the chirp of insects and the running of water.

Watched over by the silent stars.

Jerry loved it in the mountains more than anything. He had just finished his first year of college in Denver and was planning on spending most of the summer camping and hiking in the Idaho wilderness. Every year since his fifth birthday he had gone camping with his family during the summer. Now he was an experienced backpacker and the wilderness didn't worry him. He thrived out here in the wilds. To him the mountains were always a safer place than any city.

Thirty yards from the campfire his girlfriend, nineteen-year-old Tina Harris, finished dipping a small pan of water out of the river. She pulled on her cotton gloves to keep warm and turned to move up the bank toward the fire. Her small flashlight sent a beam cutting through the dark at the trail ahead as she picked her way over the rocks and tree roots toward the glow of the fire.

She stood five six, with short brown hair and large brown eyes. She was usually called cute and had hated that until last year, when it dawned on her she wouldn't be cute for too much longer. She had also just finished her first year of college in Denver and, like Jerry, was looking forward to the summer. She loved camping, but not with the passion Jerry had. She hoped later in the summer, when the mountains got really hot, to talk him into just staying at home around her parents' swimming pool in Portland, Oregon. But, on this third night into the Idaho mountains, she was happy right where she was. Tomorrow they'd reach the first hot springs and, if she knew Jerry, they'd camp there for a few days while he fished. She didn't mind. For her there was nothing like sitting in a natural hot spring under a sky full of stars.

As she neared their camp, and the light from their fire lit the trail, she shut off the flashlight. Tonight their small camp filled a flat area between a half dozen tall pine trees on a rock shelf twenty feet over the river. They had set up their tent between two of the trees and had laid out mats near the fire in an open area so they could stare at the sky.

"Problems?" Jerry asked without turning to look at her.

"Nope," she said. She set her pan of water off to one side and dropped down beside Jerry. Above her the stars now almost filled the sky. Later, when the campfire died down and the last of the sunset had vanished from the tops of the ridges, she knew the stars would paint the heavens almost pure silver.

She slipped her hand into Jerry's hand and neither of them said a word as they lay watching the sky and listening to the river. A peaceful night in the mountains, miles away from any college exams. At that moment, for both of them, life was about as good as it could get. They were young, had their health, and both had rich enough parents that they didn't have to work in the summer.

Tina squeezed Jerry's hand lightly, then suddenly sat up straight. Something was moving above them. "Jerry? Did you see—"

"Yeah," he said. He was already sitting, staring up between the trees. "Must have been an owl."

"If that was an owl, it was huge," Tina said.

Like a fast-moving cloud, a blackness crossed overhead, blocking out the stars and seeming to dull even the light from the campfire.

"Is that a storm?" Jerry asked. "I didn't hear any thunder in the valley."

"Neither did I," Tina said.

Both teenagers scrambled to their feet, never taking their eyes off the sky above them. The sound of the river faded into the distance, and the fire didn't crackle. There was no shape to the blackness and neither of them heard a sound. Just suddenly the stars and the tops of the mountains around them were blocked out as if someone had tossed a dark blanket over the trees.

Jerry turned and grabbed his flashlight from where he'd placed it on a rock. He clicked it on and pointed it into the sky, but the beam seemed to be sucked into the blackness.

"What's happening?" Jerry asked.

Tina shook her head. His voice sounded deadened, as though he was talking through a blanket. Her throat felt too dry to answer. This wasn't possible. Stars just didn't disappear from the sky.

"Let's get out of here," Jerry said. Pulling on Tina's arm he shined the light between the trees and started back toward the main trail that led up the river. Without packs they'd have a long, cold night and an even longer day tomorrow before they reached a ranger station, but Tina knew they'd make it. At the moment that was the least of her worries. What was above them was the problem.

They had only gone a few steps when the blackness of night turned to the brightness of day as an intense white light covered them, freezing them into position.

"What—" Jerry managed to say before he could say nothing more.

The last thing Tina felt was a numbing, tingling sensation, as if a dentist had given her too much Novocain. Something unseen was holding her in a standing position. She wanted to drop to the ground as the trees around her spun, but she couldn't. She fought the trapped feeling for the seconds before she passed out.

Unconscious, Jerry and Tina floated into the sky, as had the embers from their fire. As they cleared the tops of the tall pine trees the artificial day vanished from the forest floor. Moments later the stars returned to their normal place above the mountains as the blackness moved up and away.

After a few minutes the crickets started chirping again and everything seemed back to normal.

A few hours later Jerry and Tina's campfire spit its last ember into the air and cooled down to faded golden coals. By morning it was cold and dead.

1

A bad forgery's the ultimate insult.

—JONATHAN GASH
FROM *THE VATICAN RIP*

JUNE 21.
PORTLAND, OREGON

The lobby of the Sundown Hotel smelled like stale cigarettes. Grime covered the front window, and yellow water stains formed patterns on the high ceiling and walls. A fan squeaked like a ticking clock as it turned slowly over the center of the room, vainly trying to move the air.

Two faded overstuffed couches faced each other across the tiny lobby beside a caged-in front desk. Two elderly men sat on the couches, saying nothing, looking at nothing. Both had long since vanished inside their own memories, returning to the present only when forced to eat or move upstairs to their tiny rooms.

Inside the wire cage a fat man smoked a short cigarette and studied the sports page of the morning paper. He wore a stained white T-shirt with a Harley insignia on the back. The few residents who could still smell called him onion man because he always smelled of onions.

The front door swung open, crashing backward into the wall, letting in the sounds of trucks and passing traffic. An elderly man with a stooped back and thinning white hair shuffled through the door pulling a worn old leather suitcase strapped onto an aluminum carrier with small wheels. Obviously the suitcase weighed more than he was able to handle, but he didn't seem to notice. He just pulled it inside as though it was a dead body, then moved slowly to close the front door.

He pulled the suitcase over to the cage, leaving a scrape mark across the dirty floor. "Room for two weeks," he said. His voice was dull, almost automatic sounding. His eyes were a flat gray and his skin seemed pasty and moist.

The onion man inside the cage dropped his paper. "Eighty bucks per week in advance."

The old man pulled out a roll of bills and handed it to the man. "Two weeks."

"Heard ya the first time." The onion man spent a moment counting the money, then nodded and slid a key through the opening in the cage. "First door at the top of the stairs. No maids. No parties." With a chopped-off laugh at his own joke, the onion man slipped the money into the drawer under the counter and picked up his newspaper.

The old man didn't even nod. He simply picked up the key, turned, grabbed the handle on the heavy suitcase carrier, and started toward the wooden stairs. Ten minutes later he had managed to bump the heavy suitcase up the stairs and into the room. After a moment he had the door locked behind him.

He left the suitcase in the middle of the room and sat down on the bed. His main job was now done.

He focused his gaze on the old leather suitcase. He must now guard the luggage. No one was to touch it. No one. He was to die stopping any attempt.

For the next six days he was to sit on the bed and stare at the suitcase without moving.

2

We're all not quite as sane as we pretend to be.

—ROBERT BLOCH
FROM *PSYCHO*

11:05 A.M. JUNE 22.
PORTLAND, OREGON

Ex-cop turned private investigator Richard McCallum was having one of "those" days.

He crouched behind his big oak desk, his ears still ringing from the gunshot. His office smelled of sulfur and there was now a fairly large round hole in the new oak paneling beside his bookshelf. He kept staring up at the hole and the more he stared, the madder he got. It had cost him over fifteen thousand hard-earned bucks to remodel this office and now Evan Toole was punching holes in it.

And too damn close to his books for comfort.

"You still back there, McCallum?" Evan asked from where he stood in McCallum's office door, his voice clearly shaking from the excitement of firing that first shot.

"Where else would I go?" McCallum said. "You think I got a tunnel back here?"

Evan laughed. "Don't you wish."

Yeah, McCallum wished he did have an escape tunnel right at that moment. He glanced at the gun in his right hand. He could put a slug in Evan easily enough, but the paperwork downtown would be hell if he did. And if he accidentally killed the guy, the paperwork and court time would keep him jammed for months. It wasn't worth it. But he didn't put the gun down. He hated paperwork, but he wasn't stupid.

Another explosion filled the office and a second hole appeared in the wall beside the first, slightly closer to the books.

"Damn it, Evan!" McCallum shouted. "You put a hole in my books and you're dead." McCallum had spent the last ten years collecting those books. All of them were mysteries, all signed by the authors. Mysteries were his passion in life and had been since he was a kid. Mysteries had been the reason he'd become a cop and the reason he'd gone on to be a private investigator.

Evan only laughed.

McCallum's ears rang from the gunfire in the small space. He adjusted his weight to keep his legs from going to sleep. McCallum was a moderately tall man, standing just over six feet. He had a well-groomed beard and mustache. At thirty-eight he was still trim and in top physical shape from running and working out in the neighborhood gym. But staying crouched behind a desk would put anyone's legs to sleep. He didn't want that to happen just in case he had to move fast. He shifted his weight again and could feel the warm sensation of blood flowing to cramped areas.

"Come on, Evan," McCallum said after the sound of the

shot quit echoing around the office. "You're not doing yourself *or my new office* any good at all."

"Just like you didn't do me any good, McCallum," Evan said from his position in the doorway. Two more shots punched holes in the new oak paneling, sending splinters and dust through the air. "I'm just paying you back is all."

Outside the window the sounds of sirens filled the streets. McCallum clutched his own gun and forced himself to stay calm, no matter how bad the ruined oak panel looked. Shooting Evan still wasn't worth the paperwork. He'd quit the police force and become a private investigator because he hated doing paperwork. As an investigator he could have his secretary do the paperwork. No point in going back to a drawerful of it now.

One more shot cut through the air and opened another hole in his oak wall, dangerously close to the books. Then McCallum heard a click as a hammer fell on an empty chamber. McCallum poked his head over the edge of the desk.

"Clip jammed, I'll bet," McCallum said. "You want me to help?"

Evan, sweating and cussing, tried to slip a new clip into his gun without much luck. His fat hands were shaking too much. His huge body filled the office door. Evan had to be at least three hundred pounds, and at the moment he was sweating like a fountain. Huge dark rings had formed on his shirt and drops of water covered his face. He clearly hadn't shaved in a few days, and even through the smell of gunpowder McCallum caught a whiff of stale garlic. It was no wonder Evan's wife had left him. The guy was a pig.

Behind Evan, in the outer office, McCallum could see the youngest of his four assistant investigators, Arthur, trying to creep up behind the big man. McCallum shook his head in disgust. That's what he got for hiring someone by the name of Arthur. The kid had guts, but no brains. He had most likely seen far too many movies. Arthur didn't weigh much more than one hundred and thirty pounds and had more freckles than Howdy Doody. What did he think he could do to a man the size of Evan? Not even a professional cowboy with a rope and spurs could wrestle that much bulk to the ground.

McCallum tried to wave Arthur back, but the kid was so intensely focused on Evan's back that he didn't see the warning. Finally McCallum stood up completely and yelled, "Arthur, you idiot. You move one more step and you're fired."

That froze the kid in his tracks just long enough for Evan to glance around, swinging his gun in Arthur's direction as he did. McCallum laughed as the kid's face went a shade of sickly white and he dove behind a secretary's desk. McCallum's yell had probably saved the kid's stupid life.

"Smart thinking," Evan said, turning back to face McCallum.

"Unlike what you're doing now," McCallum said, still standing even though Evan's gun was now pointed at him. "You think plugging holes all over my walls is going to bring your wife back to you? I told you I never take divorce cases and this," McCallum said, pointing at the ruined oak wall, "is one good reason why. Do you know how much these new oak walls cost me?"

Evan looked as if he might cry for a moment as he waved the gun around. McCallum kept behind his desk, ready to duck for cover just in case Evan had gotten the new clip in right.

"If you'd have just taken my case," Evan said, his voice a pathetic whine, "it might have saved my marriage."

"Evan," McCallum said softly, putting as much understanding behind his words as he could, considering the circumstances. "Doris had already moved in with a golf pro down at Columbia Edgewater Country Club. She wasn't coming back. It didn't take a detective to know that."

McCallum managed not to add that a few more showers and losing about one hundred pounds might have helped get Evan's wife back, too. As W. Somerset Maugham said of his main character in his book *The British Agent*: "It was Ashenden's principle to tell as much of the truth as he conveniently could."

McCallum used that principle often.

Evan looked for a moment as if he was going to start firing again, then his arm went limp at his side, the gun pointing downward at the empty shells littering the carpet. "I'm so damn stupid."

McCallum nodded his agreement, but didn't say it out loud. He had a lot of basic principles and one of them was never calling a man with a gun stupid, even if the guy *had* said it first.

McCallum moved slowly around from behind his desk and took the pistol from Evan's hand. He patted the large man on his soft, damp shoulder as the front door to the office opened and the police stormed in. McCallum handed the lead officer Evan's gun, moved back to his desk and put his own gun away.

"Just in the nick of time, as always, I see," Detective Henry Greer said, smiling at McCallum as he squeezed past Evan and into the office. Henry and McCallum had gone through the police academy together and had been partners for ten years before McCallum left the force. Henry stood all of five six, weighed fifty pounds more than McCallum, and hated paperwork almost as much as McCallum. Henry's passion in life was doughnuts, and he planned someday to quit police work and start his own doughnut shop. Henry had three kids and an almost perfectly round wife while McCallum had no kids and was divorced. They had been best friends for years and almost always had lunch together.

Henry motioned for a uniformed officer to take the now-handcuffed Evan away, then turned back to McCallum, who turned around to stare at the holes in his wall. Way too close to his autographed books. Way too close.

"So what pulled his chain?" Henry asked.

"I wouldn't take his case," McCallum said.

"Nice job remodeling," Henry said, dropping down into the chair facing McCallum's oak desk. "I especially like the bullet hole effect."

McCallum didn't laugh.

"Honest," Henry said. "I think you should clean up the dust and leave it just like that. Give your clients something to think about."

McCallum stared at the holes for a moment, then turned and sat down in his chair. He was still trying to get his heart slowed down to near normal pace. It had been years since someone fired a gun at him.

"The investigating business must be really profitable these days," Henry said, leaning back and putting his feet up on McCallum's desk. "Hired a new assistant, remodeled the office, *and* turned down work. Life must be good."

McCallum frowned at his best friend. "As Ruth Rendell said in her book *A Judgment in Stone*, 'Some say life is the thing, but I prefer reading.' "

"Yeah," Henry said. "And I prefer doughnuts. And you're buying lunch."

3

An unwillingness to believe in impending danger is a very human quality.

—HOWARD FAST
(WRITING AS E. V. CUNNINGHAM)
FROM *THE CASE OF THE POISONED ECLAIRS*

12:56 P.M. JUNE 22.
SEATTLE, WASHINGTON

Neda Foster took a deep breath to force herself to relax slightly, then pushed open the huge oak door to her father's office suite. An unsmiling, gray-suited Secret Service man stood in front of Neda's favorite Schefflera, almost as if he were guarding it instead of the vice president in her father's inner office.

The only other person in the outer office was her father's executive secretary, Mrs. Joyce Crane, who looked up and smiled without saying a word.

Neda walked up to the Secret Service man and looked him straight in his blue eyes. "Excuse me a moment, please."

A slight look of confusion passed across the man's face. Neda knew she was an imposing figure to this man. And any man. She stood slightly over six feet, with a solid build. She had long blond hair that she kept pulled back tight in a long ponytail. And she always wore the best clothes. At the moment she had on a blue pants suit with a loose-fitting jacket over a silk blouse. But what most men found imposing was her ability to radiate her will. With a look she could make people sweat and jump into action. And when her anger boiled there was no getting in her way.

Neda smiled at the Secret Service man's confused look and made a motion with her hand for him to move to the left.

Hesitantly he did so and she said, "Thank you." Then she gently moved the leaves of the huge plant around, looking for anything she could do to help it grow. She'd given the plant to her father when she was twelve, and she and Mrs. Crane had managed to keep it alive and growing for the last eighteen years. It now stood taller than any person and occupied an entire corner of her father's plush outer office. It was a ritual that when she went downtown to her father's office she always stopped and spent an extra minute with the plant, picking off dead leaves and just basically giving it some attention. And just because the vice president of the United States was waiting for her, that was no reason to change her habit. Besides, it calmed her.

After a short pause she had picked off one dead leaf. She dropped it into the plant's huge pot and turned, nodding her thanks to the Secret Service man.

Mrs. Joyce Crane smiled formally at Neda from behind her always-neat oak desk. Joyce had been Grant Foster's right hand for longer than Neda had been alive. And since Neda's real mother had died when she was two, Neda considered Joyce more like a mother than a secretary. But with the Secret Service man standing so solemn and watching them, they both reverted to their roles of rich daughter and father's secretary.

"They're waiting for you," Mrs. Crane said in her formal voice. Then she raised her right eyebrow at Neda and gave her a little smile.

Neda smiled back. "Thank you, Mrs. Crane."

At that both of them snickered. Out of the corner of her eye Neda noticed the Secret Service man didn't even raise an eyebrow.

With a smile at Joyce, Neda pushed open the door to her father's private office.

Her father, his stylish long gray hair perfectly combed, sat behind his huge desk. He was leaning back, his hands on the arms of his chair. Neda knew that to be a guarded, but relaxed position. When he saw her he broke into a huge smile and stood.

The man sitting with his back to her also stood and turned around. She instantly recognized the tall, trim figure of Alan Wallace, the vice president.

He extended his hand. "I've been looking forward to meeting you," he said, smiling his best political smile.

Neda wanted to say, *I'll bet you are, since I'm the daughter of your richest supporter*. But instead she only smiled, took his hand, and said, "Nice to meet you, sir."

He laughed as his firm grasp held her hand for just a moment too long. "No sir-stuff with me," he said. "At least not in here. My name's Alan. Please?"

She released his hand, nodding. "All right. Alan it is."

"Good," he said, continuing his biggest smile.

Neda could see why this guy was getting all the press. He was charming, handsome in a rugged way, had a warm smile, and his gray eyes could bore a hole through you.

Neda caught herself staring at him a little too long. If he

wasn't happily married, Neda might actually have been interested. And that thought gave her a start. These days, with all that was going on in the lab and around the world, she had no time for relationships, especially a new one.

Her father pointed to the chair beside where the vice president had been sitting, and without another word they all took their places. Neda smiled at Alan and he smiled back. Then her father began talking.

Neda knew exactly what was coming next. She and her father and Joyce had practiced it twenty times, going over every possibility. But all the practice hadn't calmed her twisting stomach.

In twenty minutes the vice president of the United States was going to leave this office thinking she and her father were both total nuts.

Or he was going to be on their side.

The survival of the human race might very well rest on the open-mindedness of Vice President Alan Wallace.

4

Misfortune can happen to anyone. Only the dead are safe from it.

—HARRY KEMELMAN
FROM *FRIDAY THE RABBI SLEPT LATE*

2:06 P.M. JUNE 22.
PORTLAND, OREGON

Richard McCallum glanced at the bullet holes above his desk before he sat down. It had been a long lunch, with Henry ribbing him about the holes in his wall. And then, after lunch, Henry was mad at him for not pressing charges against Evan Toole. McCallum could see no point in going through all the hassle of pressing charges. Evan had money and he was going to pay for the repairs, plus some. Of that McCallum had no doubt. But pressing criminal charges, and getting messed up with all the paperwork doing so entailed, just wasn't worth it. Besides, Evan might not willingly pay for all the repairs if McCallum pressed charges.

McCallum took a deep breath as he sat down and forced himself to focus on the problems at hand. Across his desk sat Arrington Harris, founder of Harris Industries. He was one of Portland's richest men. He was totally bald, with a pure white mustache and white eyebrows. He wore an expensive three-piece suit, but his tie was crooked and he looked very tired.

McCallum knew why. Everyone in Portland knew why. Harris and his daughter had been making the headlines in the *Oregonian* over the last week.

It seemed his daughter, Tina, had disappeared while on a camping trip into the Idaho primitive area with her boyfriend. At this point, from what McCallum could gather from the newspaper, the leads had all dried up and all the searches had been called off.

The girl had supposedly vanished three or four days ago, just a short time before three other hikers found their abandoned camp. McCallum figured the two kids' bodies would wash up ten miles down the river any day now. They had probably gone for a late-night swim and gotten washed away by the cold river. That's the way it usually happened.

"Mr. McCallum," Arrington Harris said as McCallum scooted his chair up to his desk. "Your firm comes highly recommended."

"Thanks," McCallum said. "Always nice to hear." And it was. He'd worked hard to make this business work over the past three years, since quitting the force. And having someone like Harris say so felt good.

Harris nodded, then took a deep breath. "Do you know about my daughter, Tina?"

McCallum put on his best comforting look and nodded. "Just the little bit I have read in the paper."

"I'm afraid," Harris said, "that there isn't much more than that."

McCallum nodded and both men sat in an uncomfortable silence for a moment. McCallum was about to break it when Harris said, "I want to hire your firm to find my daughter."

McCallum sat back, staring at Harris. He would have guessed that request was coming. In fact, if he had been a betting man he would have wagered on it the moment Harris made the appointment. But McCallum doubted there was much he could do to help.

McCallum studied Harris. The man's grief at losing his daughter was being held just below the surface. That much was clear. And at the moment McCallum figured there wasn't much reason to bring that grief out. He was sure that would come when they found the girl's body. Right now Harris was a father doing everything he could to find his daughter. And coming here was just one of those things.

"Before I decide I can help," McCallum said, "I need you to tell me everything you know about Tina's disappearance, starting right from where you think the beginning is."

Harris nodded and took a deep, almost gulping breath that seemed to settle him a little. "She was camping along the Middle Fork of the Salmon River in Idaho with her boyfriend, Jerry Rodale. Her mother and I were both worried about her going into the wilderness like that, but Tina was an experienced camper and so, from what I could find out, was Jerry."

"Tell me about this Jerry?" McCallum asked.

Harris shrugged. "Not much to tell. He and Tina met last year in Denver at college. He comes from a good Denver family who are just as crazed over this thing as we are. He was never in any trouble with the law, had good grades, and seemed clean-cut and polite. To be honest, the two times I met him I really liked the kid, and both my wife and I hoped Tina would stick with him."

"Thanks," McCallum said. He made a note on his pad with Jerry Rodale's name. By tomorrow afternoon he'd know more about Jerry Rodale than Jerry's parents did. But his gut told him Tina's disappearance had nothing to do with Jerry. But he'd check out Jerry just in case. As William Marshall said in his book *Thin Air*, "Chance discoveries favor those with a prepared mind."

McCallum nodded for Harris to continue.

"Tina had been gone only four days when we got a call from the Idaho State Police. Our daughter's things, including all her camping equipment and clothes, had been found abandoned."

"Was how it was found described to you?" McCallum knew he would read the official report, but having Harris describe it might add something the police missed.

Harris shook his head no. "I actually saw it. And there are police photographs of the camp, too."

McCallum's puzzled frown made Harris quickly go on. "I flew into the area by helicopter. They had to land me a half mile upriver from the camp and I walked down to it. The police said nothing had been touched."

Harris seemed to shudder thinking about the camp, then went on. "Everything looked so normal. Their tent was up, a fire had been built, and two mats were laid out near the fire in an open area. There was a pan of water near the tent and their packs and food were stacked in a very orderly fashion. It looked as if they had already had dinner. It was as if they had simply been there one moment and vanished the next."

"No clothes down by the river?" McCallum asked.

"No," Harris said, sounding almost relieved when he said the word. "We checked. And there have been over a hundred boatloads of rafters past that point going down the river since that day. The river level is not high at the moment. If Tina and Jerry had fallen in the river they'd have been found by now."

McCallum nodded. It had been tough for Harris to talk like that about his daughter. That was clear. Maybe there was more to this disappearance than McCallum had thought from the newspapers.

"Look, Mr. McCallum," Harris said. "I know my daughter is still alive, somewhere. I can feel it. You know. Parent to child bond. I can't explain it any other way."

Every parent looking for a lost child said that exact phrase at one time or another. Ninety-five percent of the time they were wrong, but McCallum just agreed with Harris.

Harris went on. "There isn't much the Idaho State Police can do at this point. And the Wilderness Search and Rescue have called off their people until a new lead comes up. I just can't let the search for my daughter stop cold now."

"What do you think I can do to help?"

Harris slouched in the chair, almost as if half the bones in his body were made of rubber. For a man of Harris's place in society, that was not a flattering position. "I really don't know," Harris said softly. "Anything is better than nothing."

McCallum stared at the man for a moment, then sighed. "All right, Mr. Harris. I'll see what I can do to find Tina."

It was as if the man's bones had suddenly gained some strength. He sat up and squared his shoulders. "Thank you," he said.

"Don't thank me yet," McCallum said. "There's work to do. And I'm going to need a lot of your help."

"Anything," Harris said. "Just tell me what. I've felt so useless since this all happened."

"First," McCallum said, "I need you to go get a stiff drink and then come back and tell a tape recorder out there in the outer office every detail you can remember of the campsite. Then I want you to tell that same tape recorder every detail you can think of about your daughter's habits, likes, and dislikes. Third, anything you know about Jerry, his family, and your observations of him. I know that won't be easy, but it needs to be done."

Harris nodded, but said nothing.

"Then," McCallum said, "by the time you finish that I will have maps of the area Tina vanished in. I want you to pinpoint on those maps exactly where Tina was when she disappeared. I need to get a sense of the area. All right?"

Harris nodded, his eyes bright with the prospect of action and the return of a little hope again.

"Also," McCallum asked, "are you up for another trip into the area?"

"If it will help," Harris said.

"It might," McCallum said. "Does your firm have its own jet?"

Harris nodded.

"Good. Have it standing by tomorrow morning at dawn. And give me the name of that helicopter service and I'll get us booked for tomorrow morning. I need to see the location of the camp."

"The jet will be ready," Harris said, standing. He reached across and shook McCallum's hand. Then, with a nod, he turned and headed for the door.

"Harris," McCallum said.

Harris stopped and turned.

"Don't forget the drink first."

Harris stared at him for a moment, then with a half smile headed for the front door.

Forcing himself to not look at the bullet holes in the oak over his desk, McCallum moved to his office door. He waited a moment for Harris to clear the front door, then shouted, "Arthur! My office. Now!"

The kid looked up from his desk, startled, like a deer caught in the headlights. His face flushed, making his freckles stand out even more.

McCallum managed not to smile before he had his back to the kid and was headed toward his chair.

5

Publicity is like power . . . it's a rare man who isn't corrupted by it.

—ANTHONY PRICE
FROM *COLONEL BUTLER'S WOLF*

3:30 P.M. JUNE 22.
PORTLAND, OREGON

Claudia Young watched as Portland Mayor Janet Osborne strode toward her. Around them the wide marble corridors of city hall buzzed with normal daily activity, the sounds of city government in action a dull roar that seemed to echo in the long halls.

Claudia leaned against a smooth stone pillar and waited for her boss. She had been Janet Osborne's assistant and right hand for the past three years and she loved her job. At least most of the time.

Right at the moment she wasn't so sure.

Janet had been very secretive about a family meeting this morning and Claudia always hated it when Janet kept secrets from her. Any secret.

And now, this afternoon, Janet had three back-to-back meetings with state senators up from Salem. Yet she had called the office and wanted to see Claudia over coffee for some "unofficial" business. "Outside the office."

The word "unofficial" made Claudia even more nervous than the "outside the office" part.

A young couple Claudia didn't recognize stopped Janet ten feet short of her. The mayor smiled her best "keep-them-all-happy" smile and nodded as the man said something to her. She had the ability to make anyone think what they were saying was the most important thing in the world. She was doing that now to this young couple.

Janet Osborne stood barely five feet tall, eight full inches shorter than Claudia. While Claudia looked tall and trim, the mayor looked powerful, with strong arms and solid legs. She had dark brown short hair that always seemed to be in perfect position, while Claudia's hair was pitch-black, long, and, more often than not, in her face.

They had originally met when Claudia interned at the state senate while attending the University of Oregon. Janet, at that time, was a freshman senator from Portland, not far out of college herself. They hit it off at once, and Claudia had been on her staff ever since graduation. Some people around Portland called Claudia "assistant mayor," but never to her face.

The mayor made the young couple laugh, then shook both their hands and made it the last ten feet to Claudia. She handed Claudia a manila folder she had been carrying and said, "Coffee. Quick."

"You're going to be late," Claudia said. "Senator Oltion won't like that."

Janet nodded. "I already had Mary call his office and

push the meeting back a half hour. The old fisherman can just stew if he wants."

Claudia glanced, half-startled, at Janet as they pushed into the building's employee lunchroom, saying hello to various people as they went. Luckily for them, it was mid-afternoon and the place was almost empty.

They both got their coffees and found a booth, with Janet sitting with her back to the room.

"You're driving me nuts, you know," Claudia said after they had both sipped their drinks. "What in the world is going on?"

Janet laughed. "Sorry, but this isn't really office business. In fact, it's more like a personal favor."

Claudia looked into Janet's eyes. She could see that Janet felt uncomfortable with the entire situation, so Claudia said, "Now you got me even more worried. What can I do?"

"Are you still seeing McCallum?"

Of all the questions from Janet that Claudia might have expected, that wasn't the one. "When our schedules match," Claudia said. "But we're not engaged or anything like that." Actually, she and McCallum had an extremely comfortable arrangement. They both had their own places, their own lives, and their own jobs. Yet each knew the other was there. Claudia usually spent one night a week at McCallum's apartment and he spent one night a week at hers. Never on any schedule. For the last few years it had just worked out that way.

Janet nodded and tapped the manila envelope she'd handed Claudia. "This is all the information I can get about a man named Albert Hancer, formerly of North Hills Rest Home."

"Okay," Claudia said. She had no idea where Janet was

heading, but she had known Janet long enough to give her time to get there.

Janet took another long sip from her coffee, then took a deep breath and faced Claudia. "Albert Hancer is my mother's step-brother. Her only brother. He would have turned seventy-eight in three days. But he's turned up missing."

"From the nursing home?" Claudia asked.

Janet nodded. "Five days ago. I was wondering if McCallum could look into it for me. I'll pay his normal rates and expenses."

Claudia stared at Janet. This wasn't like Janet at all. Normally, if she wanted something done, Claudia and the rest of the staff would have to hold her back from doing it herself. She could have picked up the phone herself and called McCallum. She didn't need to go through Claudia. Unless . . .

"There's more, isn't there?" Claudia asked.

Janet nodded and, for the first time in their relationship, Claudia saw her friend look embarrassed. "We've got to keep my name out of this. No one knows Albert was a relative of mine. Hell, I only met the man twice."

Claudia nodded, not really understanding, but letting Janet finish.

"And," Janet said, "there's some unexplained stuff with the disappearance."

"Kidnapped?" Claudia asked. "Murdered?"

Janet gave a half laugh. "No. But four witnesses, two of them nurses, swear he was taken up into a spaceship."

Janet's gaze bored into Claudia until finally Claudia could take it no longer. She started to laugh. After a moment, between laughs she said, "You've got to be kidding?"

Janet, who had also started to laugh slightly, shook her head no. "Very serious."

Claudia managed to stop laughing and think. Janet was absolutely correct. Her name had to stay away from Albert Hancer's disappearance. The press would have a field day if the mayor's family ever got linked with a UFO close encounter.

Claudia took the envelope and tucked it into her briefcase. "I'll get McCallum to look into it."

"He's famous for not liking city hall," Janet said. "Can he keep his mouth shut on this?"

Claudia laughed. "Of that, you have no worry. He'll keep quiet. He's a full professional at his job." She took a drink of her coffee and then smiled at Janet. "Especially if he ever wants to get laid again."

Janet looked at Claudia for a moment with a look of shock before breaking out into howling laughter. Heads turned to stare around the lunchroom as the two women laughed together.

Thirty minutes later Claudia called McCallum and set up a dinner date. On her.

Actually, it would be on the mayor, but Claudia figured McCallum didn't need to know that until later.

6

First you dream, then you die.

—CORNELL WOOLRICH
FROM HIS NOTEBOOKS

7:48 P.M. JUNE 22.
LOCATION UNKNOWN

Tina Harris forced herself to keep her eyes closed and think about the peacefulness of the river and their camp under the stars. She could feel a rough surface under her back. Rough and gritty. What would cause that? She must have rolled off her sleeping pad during the night. That's what had happened. She'd had a nightmare and rolled off her sleeping pad. Jerry would laugh at her, sleeping on the ground when she could have been sleeping on an air-filled pad.

Around her it was hot. Almost stiflingly hot. The morning sun must be hitting the tent, making it too warm. That happened once in a while, but usually the warmth of the sun felt good after a cold night in the mountains.

But it was too hot. The ground under her too rough. She knew she wasn't in their tent above the Middle Fork of the Salmon River. She knew Jerry wasn't beside her, snoring lightly as he always did. But she desperately wanted to believe he was.

She wanted to believe that she'd had a nightmare and nothing more.

She rolled over slightly. She could feel only rough dirt, warm under her shoulder and arm. No familiar feel of sleeping bag or tent bottom. No familiar rustle of nylon tent fabric. The hope of a nightmare vanished and a few flickering memories returned.

She could remember being frozen beside Jerry by a white light coming down through the trees. She could remember fighting not to pass out and losing.

She could remember waking up on a hospital-like table, with a white light over her, a light so bright it blinded her. Then there was pain so intense everything went black.

She also had a faint, dream-like memory of waking up inside a black cavern, filled with coughing and crying people. And she could remember a smell, as though an outhouse had been tipped over and she was lying in the middle of the mess. A choking, awful smell made worse by the heat. It had gotten so bad that the smell finally forced her back into unconsciousness.

Now she was awake again. The smell was still smothering her, but somehow it seemed less, as if she had gotten used to it in her sleep.

And it didn't seem quite so hot.

Carefully she forced her eyes open.

For a moment she thought she was blind. Nothing but blackness greeted her. Then shapes formed in the blackness.

Shapes lying close to her on the ground. A few human shapes sitting nearby.

A long thin streak of brightness overhead was the only light.

Her head spinning slightly, she pushed herself up into a sitting position, blinking to get her eyes to focus. It was the feel of dirt against her legs and bottom that made her realize she was naked. Totally naked.

And from the crusty feeling along her legs and butt, she had wet herself while she slept.

A sudden massive embarrassment overwhelmed her and she covered herself as best she could with her hands. Then, as her eyes adjusted even more to the faint light, she saw that those around her were also naked. And no one was looking at her. Most of those around her were beyond caring if they were naked or not.

Some of them weren't moving.

Some weren't breathing.

She forced herself to take a deep breath, take her gaze off those nearest her, and look around the full room. From what she could tell, she was in a cave. The floor was dirt and rock and the walls appeared to be lava rock. The light source was a crack a few feet long in the high ceiling. She guessed at least fifty, maybe closer to a hundred, naked people were scattered around the room and she could hear a few of them talking softly. A few others moaned or cried quietly to themselves.

At the moment she felt like crying also, but somehow managed to choke it down inside. She made herself focus on the face of a man lying nearby. He wasn't Jerry.

Quickly, she checked the others around her, hoping against all hope that Jerry would be close. But he wasn't.

Only unconscious humans scattered like so much wood around the cave.

Two women and a man were sitting on rocks against one wall of the room. They seemed to be in better shape than anyone else. Tina pushed herself to her feet and started in their direction, stepping over and around humans in the near dark. She didn't allow herself to look at the people beyond checking to see if each body was Jerry. But it was clear many of them were either dead or near death. A number of times her foot found something wet on the floor and she forced herself not to think about what it might be.

As she neared the three people sitting on the rocks, they stopped talking and turned to face her. Both women seemed to be about ten years older than she was, from what she could tell in the near dark. The man looked to be at least sixty, but in pretty good shape. As with everyone else, all three were totally naked.

The only thing she could think to say to them was, "Where are we?"

One of the women, her hair cut short, shook her head slowly. "We wish we knew." Her voice sounded strong, as if she was used to answering questions.

Tina faced them, her hands clasped in front of her. The room felt as if it were still spinning. The woman with short hair must have noticed. She pointed to a rock. "Sit down before you fall down. It's going to get dark in here soon enough. No point in wasting too much of your energy while it's still so warm."

Tina gladly sat, ignoring the pain of the rough stone. The room seemed to stop spinning a little, enough for her to look at the three facing her.

The other woman, who had long hair and a very thin body, asked, "Where are you from?"

Tina sniffled, then managed to hold back from bursting into tears. "Portland."

"Oregon?" the short-haired woman asked.

"Yes," Tina said.

"Where were you taken?" the older man asked.

"Taken?"

The guy laughed softly, but it wasn't mocking. More of an *I understand* laugh. "Where were you when the white light knocked you out?"

"Central Idaho Primitive Area. I was camping with my boyfriend, Jerry. I need to find him." Tina glanced around at the rock cave full of humans.

The woman with short hair reached out and patted Tina's knee. "Give yourself a few minutes to rest. Then after it cools down in here a little more I'll help you look. But I don't expect he's here. They usually don't allow people who are taken together to stick together."

The other two nodded in agreement.

"They?" Tina asked.

"The aliens," the woman said. "Haven't you seen them?"

The word *aliens* echoed in Tina's head as the memory of the white operating room came back. And the faces behind the white light.

Snake-like, evil faces.

Alien faces.

7

Every woman from daily help to the Queen of England can gauge a man quicker than a flea can hop.

—NIGEL MORLAND
FROM *A ROPE FOR THE HANGING*

9:16 P.M. JUNE 22.
PORTLAND, OREGON

Richard McCallum stared at Claudia. She was dressed in a striking black pantsuit, her black hair long and full around her head and down over her bare shoulders. She had a pearl necklace around her neck and matching pearl earrings. Dressed to kill and very much out of place in the ice cream parlor they now sat in. Even the pimple-faced kid behind the counter had stared at her between making their sundaes.

Two hours ago she'd taken him to his favorite Hunan restaurant and even bought drinks. There was no doubt she wanted something from him. They'd been going together, "dating" as they both liked to call it, for over three years and he knew her well enough to know when she wanted something.

And she knew how to get it from him. She was doing that tonight. As Dashiell Hammett had Sam Spade say in *The Maltese Falcon*, for this "I don't mind a reasonable amount of trouble."

After dinner McCallum and Claudia had walked hand-in-hand down near the river to their favorite little shop for ice cream, enjoying the beautiful summer evening. Now they were just finishing dessert and she still hadn't sprung her question. It was starting to bother him.

She pushed her empty sundae dish to the center of the table and sighed. "That was wonderful."

He'd finished his dish a full minute before. "That it was," he agreed.

There was a long moment of silence as they both stared out into the summer night and over the peaceful river. It was one of those perfect summer nights in Portland. Couples walked along the bank and a group of teenagers sprawled on a park lawn near the shore. There were three other couples in the parlor with them at the moment, but they were all far enough away that they couldn't hear them talking.

Finally Claudia said, "Aren't you wondering what I want?"

He looked at the slight grin on her face and laughed. "If you really want to know, I've been wondering since you called, and it's been killing me for the last hour. I would have bet you'd have gotten to it over coffee at the restaurant."

She laughed. "See, you don't know me as well as you thought you did." She squeezed his hand, then reached down into her purse and brought out a manila envelope. She tossed it over the ice cream dishes in front of him and then glanced around as if she'd done something wrong and hoped she hadn't been caught.

"Is this hot?" McCallum asked, pointing at the envelope without touching it.

"No," Claudia said, and then laughed again. But this time the laugh was forced and they both knew it. So she went on. "It's a favor for the mayor. A missing persons' case. I told her I'd see if you'd look into it. She'll pay your full rates and all expenses."

"And she doesn't want anyone to know her involvement, right?"

Claudia nodded. "You'll understand why when you read what's in there."

He still hadn't touched the envelope and wasn't certain yet if he was going to. "Want to give me some basics?"

Claudia nodded. "The mayor's stepuncle disappeared from a nursing home on the north side. She really doesn't know the man and there's no connection to her at all." Claudia pointed to the envelope. "That's everything Janet had about him, as well as the police report on his disappearance."

"So why have me look into it when she's got an entire police force at her beck and call?"

Claudia glanced around again. One of the couples was standing to leave and Claudia actually waited until they were outside before she leaned across the table and whispered, "Supposedly he was abducted by aliens."

McCallum couldn't help the burst of laughter. He tried to hold it, but it was one of those laughs that just couldn't be held back. And after it was out, he couldn't stop it.

But Claudia only smiled at him. And her smile was not a happy one.

After taking a deep breath McCallum leaned forward. "You're serious, aren't you?"

"The mayor is," Claudia said, the smile dropping from her face. "It might be her job, and mine, on the line here. Especially if the press got hold of this."

McCallum shook his head, still laughing to himself. The mayor's stepuncle abducted by aliens out of a nursing home. This was too much for even the craziest scam artists. But it sure was funny.

Again he broke into light laughter and managed to contain it back to chuckles after a few seconds.

Claudia on the other hand was not amused.

Finally he shrugged at her and opened up the envelope. He glanced at the details for the lost stepuncle, then flipped to the police report. Four different witnesses said they saw basically the same thing: The guy was covered in a white light and lifted into the sky, into a dark shape hovering there. One of the witnesses was the night charge nurse, an RN who most likely put her job on the line with such a story.

McCallum slid the papers back into the envelope and closed it. Then he looked up into Claudia's stern face. "So what exactly does her highness want me to do?"

"Just make some discreet inquiries, see what you can find, and keep your mouth shut. She's doing it for her mother."

"Full rates," McCallum said. "Okay, tell your boss she has hired an investigator."

Now Claudia smiled, a very large and very real smile. "Thanks."

"No, thank you," McCallum said, smiling. "I can always use the business."

Claudia reached across the table and placed her hand on his. "Too bad you're leaving so early in the morning." Her smile would have melted a glacier.

"Oh," he said. "It's not *that* early."

She laughed, grabbed his hand, and pulled him to his feet. "Good. Plan on sleeping on the plane."

And the next morning that's exactly what he did. All the way to central Idaho.

8

No one wants to be part of a fiction, and even less so if that fiction is real.

—PAUL AUSTER
FROM *THE LOCKED ROOM*

7:30 A.M. JUNE 23.
BELLINGHAM, WASHINGTON

Neda Foster held the door open and motioned for the vice president to step through.

"John," Vice President Alan Wallace said to the Secret Service man walking slightly to one side of him. "Wait here."

"But sir, we—"

"I'm only going in this lab," Wallace said. "I want you to wait right here. I won't be that long."

John glanced at the open door which led into an airlock-like small room, then nodded.

Neda was impressed. From her experience and understanding, presidents and vice presidents had a very tough time controlling the Secret Service men around them. Alan did it without hesitation and they did what he said.

She nodded to the vice president as he went past her. The presentation she and her father had made to him had broken his initial shell of doubts. He'd changed his schedule and stayed overnight in Seattle, for the sole purpose of viewing their lab this morning. She knew that he wasn't totally convinced that what she and father had said was true. No totally sane person could be, no matter how much the evidence pointed in one direction. But she knew without a doubt that, after this morning, he would be completely on their side.

She and her father and the vice president had spent the rest of the evening talking over dinner. And later drinks. The more time she spent with Alan Wallace, the more impressed she was with the man. And very glad he was joining their cause.

She closed the outer door behind them and punched a code into a panel near the inner door. After a moment the door clicked and opened quietly.

She stepped inside a few paces and then moved sideways so the vice president could see the entire room in front of him. The place still gave her the chills and she knew how it affected others. Shock.

And sometimes pure terror.

Followed by complete loyalty to the cause. The main display was designed for just that purpose.

Actually, the room was nothing more than a large warehouse converted into a combination modern lab and control center. The floors, walls, and ceilings had been painted pure white. Hundreds of lab tables formed groups around the room. Some tables were covered with parts of machines. Others were filled with computers. At the moment about thirty people were at work around the room, yet it still seemed mostly empty of life.

The center of the room was filled with a huge global map surrounded by computers and cluttered desktops. Neda's desk was near that map, where she could run everything going on around her.

However, it wasn't the maps and the desks and the painted walls that always struck visitors first. It was the two gigantic statues of the alien Klar that occupied an elevated platform against the far wall.

The statues were of two Klar standing side by side.

Neda and her father had the two statues built using descriptions Neda and others who had seen the aliens gave the artist. The two statues were as close as anyone could get to what the Klar really looked like. Height, weight, everything.

Those two giants pieces of plaster always made Neda shudder. This morning was no different.

Neda used the alien statues shamelessly to recruit help. She would use them to recruit the vice president of the United States for the team working to fight the real aliens out there. The statues, combined with the previous night's presentation and six notebooks full of documentation would do the trick.

Both Klar statues were over eight feet tall, with hoof-like feet. Viewers' first impression was that they were snake-like. They had two intense black eyes and two slits below the eyes that appeared to be nostrils. Their mouths slanted downward in slashes that extended down onto their wide necks.

Their heads were cone-shaped and positioned forward of their bodies on thick, wide necks. Their necks were cords of thick muscles, far wider than their heads, which gave them a cobra-like look. Their "skin" was a scale-like brown-and-white substance that formed intricate patterns. They had four arms, the two major ones extending from the huge neck muscles and ending in four claw-like fingers. The two smaller arms were tucked under the larger ones and also ended in four claws.

Both wore a tight-fitting form of elastic uniform. Both appeared to be of the same sex. One alien held a rifle-like gun in its two large arms, aiming it out over the room.

The vice president's mouth dropped open for a moment as he stared at the statues, then he closed it and swallowed hard. After a moment he moved toward them slowly, talking as he went. "Where did you get them? Is this actually what the Klar look like? How did you have them made?"

Neda laughed. Even the vice president asked the normal questions. She moved up past him and stood in front of the two statues. "These two," Neda said, pointing at the statues, "are the best representations we can come up with of the two Klar I saw when I was abducted."

The vice president's head snapped around and he looked at her. "I didn't know."

She laughed. "Very few people do. And I was one of the lucky few that have gotten away."

Neda could tell that he desperately wanted to ask more questions of her, but thought better of it. Later, if she had the chance, she'd tell him her story.

He looked back up at the statues towering over the room.

"They are real Klar in every detail we've been able to piece together. Over sixteen hundred people have stood here just as you are this morning and looked at these two statues of the aliens. Every person who has seen them is now working for us in one way or another."

"Working?" Again the vice president pulled his gaze

away from the two Klar statues to glance at her. "Doing what?"

"Another long story," she said. "But first, sir, take a good look at them. Imagine yourself stretched out on a table, unable to move, being studied by those two. Then come and sit down. We've got a lot to talk about in a very short time."

He nodded, then turned and stared at the two Klar statues. Then, with one word—"Creepy"—he moved over and sat down across from her desk.

"What's the first question you have at this moment?" Neda said. "I'll try to answer it and then outline what we are doing to stop those creatures."

The vice president glanced back at the two alien statues. Then he turned back to Neda. "I didn't ask this last night, but do you know how long they've been here, on Earth? Studying us? And where did the name Klar come from?"

Neda nodded. "We have a pretty good guess. At least fifty years. And they've just always been called Klar by humans. We're not sure exactly why."

The vice president's face went white, then he nodded.

With that movement Neda began to outline what the sixteen hundred people working for her were doing. And where they needed his help.

9

If you know anything about detective work, you'd know that the most seemingly impossible conditions are often the easiest to explain.

—CAROLYN WELLS
FROM *VICKY VAN*

9:20 A.M. JUNE 23.
CENTRAL IDAHO PRIMITIVE AREA

The flight from Portland to the little resort community of McCall, Idaho, had been quick as far as McCallum was concerned. He'd kicked back the wide chair, put up his feet, and slept from the moment the wheels of the Harris Industries jet left the runway in Oregon to the moment they touched down in Idaho.

Harris told McCallum later that he had managed to do a little business during the flight and McCallum had no idea what his freckled assistant Arthur had done. But when McCallum woke up the kid's face looked a little pale and he wasn't talking much at all. Maybe the flight had been bumpy. McCallum had been far, far too sound asleep to even notice. Thanks to Claudia and her unusual hiring-an-investigator methods.

Valley County Sheriff Bill Holt met them as they got off the plane. He was a solid, friendly man with a big smile, a thick black mustache, and a small pot belly that hung over his wide belt. He wore a brown uniform and a wide-brimmed hat. McCallum knew from the reports that he'd worked with the state police on the Harris case, and Mr. Harris actually seemed glad to see him again.

Short introductions, a transfer of a few bags of supplies from the jet, and ten minutes after leaving the corporate jet they were airborne again, only this time in a helicopter with the words BACK COUNTRY AVIATION stamped on the doors.

The pilot, a middle-aged guy named Tom, swung the chopper around and headed it at an upward slant toward the top of the mountain range in the distance, barely clearing a telephone pole as he did.

McCallum had taken the front seat, with the sheriff and Harris in the back seats and Arthur half-kneeling, half-sitting in the luggage area behind them. It wasn't McCallum's first time in a helicopter, but the way Tom sort of aimed the thing at the top of the mountain ridge gave him an uneasy feeling. There were far too many reports of small planes and helicopters crashing against high mountains for him to like having one he was riding in aimed at a mountain.

McCallum forced himself to relax, wake up, and look around a little. The roar of the helicopter's engines was a steady background noise and made almost any form of talking impossible. So the only thing there was to do was look at the countryside below. And there was plenty to look at.

The day was beautiful, with crystal-clear air and only a few fluffy white clouds floating through the bright blue sky. Tom, in the only full sentence he'd uttered before they left the ground had said, "It'll be a hot one."

The valley they were climbing out of was postcard-stunning in its beauty. A river wandered through the green fields and a crystal-blue lake filled one end. The little town of McCall crowded against one side of the lake and McCallum could see houses strung along the lake shore in the pine trees, tiny fingers of docks poking into the blue water. Right at this moment he would have much rather been sitting on one of those docks reading a good mystery, with Claudia sunning herself beside him.

Strips of bare ground cut through the trees of a tall mountain to the north of the lake, marking it as a ski hill. He could see the poles of the chairlifts dotting the hill. All in all, McCall was a beautiful place. McCallum decided that if he ever got the time he and Claudia *would* come over here for a vacation. It certainly looked relaxing enough. He'd bring a few books to read, and they might even be able to find some country bar to go dancing one night. It would be a fun trip.

Tom took them over the top of the mountain ridge about two hundred feet above the tree tops and the snow drifts and then leveled out.

McCallum glanced over at the altimeter. Eight thousand three hundred feet. McCallum would have been much happier with a few hundred feet or so more height over those trees, but he didn't say anything. Clearly Tom knew exactly what he was doing and had most likely done it hundreds of times.

At least McCallum hoped he had. If this was Tom's first flight McCallum didn't want to know about it.

Ahead, and in all directions, McCallum could see nothing but mountains. Ridgelines disappeared in the clear distance in front of them like waves on an ocean. Snow-covered peaks jutted into the sky far higher than the helicopter was at the moment. McCallum always knew this area was huge, but until this very moment he had no idea just how vast it really was.

And below them not a building or road in sight. It was as if humans didn't really belong here.

Maybe they didn't.

McCallum pushed that thought right back where it came from.

Over the next fifteen minutes Tom skirted close to the tops of three more ridgelines. One moment the chopper would be three thousand feet over a valley floor and the next it would seem to clip the tops of the trees on the ridge. Finally, after barely clearing one rock- and tree-covered peak, the chopper turned to the left and dropped down into a valley.

"Sulfur Creek!" Tom shouted over the sound of the chopper, pointing at a faint blue ribbon winding through the trees below. "We'll follow it down to the Middle Fork!"

McCallum only nodded, not bothering to try to shout back. From the look of the headphones Tom wore, he would have had to read McCallum's lips to hear him anyway.

McCallum leaned over and stared at the small creek below. If that was Sulfur Creek, then he knew they were smack over the largest primitive area in the lower forty-eight states. He'd studied the map of the area enough to know that Sulfur Creek dumped into the Middle Fork of the Salmon River about three miles above where Tina Harris and Jerry Rodale had disappeared.

McCallum stared into the distance to his right. In that direction the resort town of Sun Valley, Idaho was about a hundred miles to the south of their location. The edge of Yellowstone Park was a hundred plus miles to the east, dead ahead, and the River of No Return was a hundred miles to the north out Tom's window.

There was nothing but dangerous mountains, rivers, and wildlife where they were now.

After a few more minutes Tom had the helicopter down a few hundred feet above the valley floor, skimming along at about sixty miles per hour. The huge mountains now towered above them as they flashed along, occasionally being jarred by an air pocket. McCallum's biggest fear at this height was of an air pocket slamming them into the trees.

"Moose!" Tom shouted, and pointed ahead.

A huge moose, its long nose pointed up at them, stood in the middle of a meadow. The thing was bigger than a horse and looked much meaner. Not even the sound of the approaching helicopter seemed to scare it.

"Stay away from them!" Tom shouted, then laughed to himself at some private joke.

McCallum had no intention of arguing with the man. Or even asking what was so funny. Moose had never struck him as funny animals, except maybe Bullwinkle.

A moment later the helicopter banked over a large blue river and headed downstream.

The Middle Fork of the Salmon River tumbled and fell over rocks below. From the air the water looked extremely rough and fast. McCallum couldn't imagine that people actually rafted that river, but they did, starting about ten miles upstream from where they were at the moment.

Three minutes later a clearing appeared near the river and Tom slowed and finally hovered, setting the helicopter down with only a slight bump in the grass between the tall, thin lodgepole pines.

Tom flicked a few dozen switches and the engine roar slowly died away, leaving McCallum's ears ringing. He was very glad they were back on solid ground. Unusually glad.

Climbing out, the first thing McCallum noticed was the heat. For some reason, flying over snow drifts and between snow-covered ridges, he'd not realized how hot it might be in the mountain valleys. But it wasn't even ten in the morning yet and this area felt damn hot. He was glad they weren't going to be in here long.

He moved away from the helicopter into some shade and waited until the others climbed out and joined him. A slight wind made a rustling sound in the trees, and the river filled the steep-walled valley with a dull, faint roar of water rushing over rocks.

"This way," the sheriff said, and started off across the meadow. They wound through a few trees before coming on a dirt trail that ran parallel with the river. The next half mile turned out to be much farther than walking a half mile in downtown Portland.

The trail climbed up and down like a yo-yo, and wasn't straight for more than twenty feet. Three times they had to either go around or climb over fallen trees. For a few hundred years the trail was on a ledge about a hundred feet over the river, then it wound down until they were beside the roaring water. Then it climbed back up into the trees.

McCallum knew that most of the people who were crazy enough to walk this trail carried heavy packs. He couldn't even imagine that. He was having trouble with the trail without carrying a thing. And he considered himself in good shape.

Finally Sheriff Holt said, panting, "Here we are." He pointed above the trail and started up into a small clearing.

"Thank God," Arthur said softly behind McCallum. McCallum actually agreed. His shirt was totally drenched with sweat and his heart was racing. He had no doubt Claudia would say it was good for him, but at the moment he wasn't so sure.

Holt stopped, turned, and handed McCallum a water bottle. "Take a good one," he said. "This heat and altitude will drain you faster than punching a hole in a water balloon."

McCallum laughed, but did as he was told, then passed the bottle to Arthur. The water was warm, but it clearly hit the spot.

McCallum glanced around. Harris was sitting on a large stone back near the trail. He had a lost look in his eyes. Arthur handed the bottle back to him and he took another drink, then passed it back. "Thanks."

"No problem," Holt said as he took a drink himself before putting the bottle back into a carrier on his belt. "I'm just glad Mr. Harris has got someone else looking at this case. It's been a real puzzle to my office and to the state police."

"I'll bet," McCallum said. "Arthur, go sit and keep Mr. Harris company."

Arthur nodded, a look of relief on his flushed face.

McCallum glanced around at the trampled earth among the trees. "Sheriff, would you mind telling me how the kids' camp was laid out? I saw the pictures, but it would be nice if you described it, too."

"Sure," Holt said. He turned and pointed at a flat area between two trees. "Their tent was pitched there, opening facing east. Any experienced backpacker tries to pitch a tent facing east to catch the morning sun."

McCallum nodded and for the next ten minutes Sheriff Holt described the camp of the two young college kids, detail by detail, sometimes mentioning how they had been doing something right in their camping skills.

McCallum listened intently, then glanced around at the valley. "So, this far into the back country, how were they ever reported missing?"

"A lot of luck," Holt said, pulling out the water bottle and taking another swig. He offered it to McCallum, who shook his head no. "Three trail workers from the Forest Service just happened past here, heading for a slide ten miles downriver. You know those three are the only ones responsible for maintaining almost a thousand miles of trails in this wilderness area? Can't be done. A few years from now most of the trails won't be passable. And except for the river or helicopter, there's no other way in or out of here."

Holt shook his head in disgust. McCallum could tell that this was a very personal subject for the man. And McCallum knew enough to not get him started on it.

"So," McCallum said, steering the conversation away from government shortfalls and back to the missing kids, "the trail crew stopped?"

Holt nodded. "Their names are in my report, but no telling where in here they are at the moment."

After seeing mountain range after mountain range from the helicopter, McCallum figured that there was no point in even trying to find the trail crew.

"They saw the camp," Holt went on, "and as they always do, they stopped to see if everyone was all right. Sort of a survival courtesy in these mountains."

"I can understand that," McCallum said.

"They found the camp just as I described it," Holt said. "They figured the occupants were off fishing or something, but the leader of the crew, a guy named Bob, said the place felt *odd*, so they took a break and hung around a while. When no one showed up in an hour Bob sent his two co-workers on to the landslide to get to work while he waited here."

"Smart guy," McCallum said.

"That he is," the sheriff said, then went on. "By late that evening it was clear that no one was returning to this camp, so Bob left a note for his workers, dropped his gear, and hightailed it back up the river to the forest ranger at Dagger Falls. About ten miles."

McCallum nodded. "So how'd they know whose camp this was?"

Holt laughed, his voice echoing through the hot air and pine trees. "Most smart folks hiking in here check in at the ranger station, or at one of the bordering ranches before they ever get near these mountains. These two kids were no dummies. They followed all the rules and checked in with the ranger at Dagger Falls. No one had started down this trail since they had."

"So what happened next?"

Holt shrugged. "Bob came back down here and started scouting the nearby area. By this time the following morning the state police and I were in here. We studied the place and then called in the state Search and Rescue. All without luck. When we called off the search two days later, we packed up their camp and hauled it out."

McCallum thanked the sheriff and then turned and walked up the hill. The slope angled upward quickly until it turned into an almost-vertical mountain wall disappearing up into the blue sky. McCallum couldn't imagine anyone going up that, for any reason. He'd only gone a hundred feet, and maybe climbed forty, and he was sweating like mad again.

He turned around and stared back down through the trees. Holt had moved down to where Mr. Harris and Arthur sat. McCallum could see the blue water of the river, and on the other side of the river almost-vertical rock-covered mountains.

No way out.

So where did those kids go?

McCallum made his way between thin pine trees and over rocks back down to the trail, sweating as he went. As he approached the group Holt again handed him the water bottle and this time McCallum didn't refuse.

"I assume the Search and Rescue people covered the mountains," McCallum asked.

"On foot where they could," Holt said. "The rest with two helicopters."

"And downriver?" McCallum asked.

Holt nodded. "All the way down to where the river empties into the main branch of the Salmon. That's about ninety miles from here, where the rafters get out. But two bodies would never make it that far this time of the year. Water's too low."

McCallum again turned and studied the surrounding area, looking for anything, any clue that would lead him to figure out where those kids went.

"It's a real puzzle, isn't it?" the sheriff said.

"That it is," McCallum said. "That it is."

There were only three ways out of this valley. The two

kids could have walked back up the trail. Or they could have gone down the trail deeper into the wilderness. Or they could have gone into the river. Only three ways.

It wasn't until McCallum was strapped into the front seat of Tom's helicopter, studying the trees dropping away below him, that it dawned on him that there was a fourth way out of this valley.

And he was taking it.

10

In former days, everyone found the assumption of innocence so easy: today we find fatally easy the assumption of guilt.

—AMANDA CROSS
FROM *POETIC JUSTICE*

3:24 P.M. JUNE 23.
PORTLAND, OREGON

Claudia smiled at the mayor as they both settled into the booth in the back of the city hall cafeteria. There was only one other occupied table, on the far side of the large room, and most of the noise came from the dishwasher in the kitchen banging pots.

"He agreed," Claudia said. "And he'll keep it confidential, as he does with all his clients."

Janet smiled back. "Good. And please, no details as to how you convinced him."

Both women laughed, then Janet turned serious. "I got a call this afternoon from the manager of North Hills Rest Home. He's the only one who knows of my relationship to Albert, and he's helping me keep it quiet on that front."

Claudia nodded, letting Janet go on.

"Two investigators from Seattle were there this morning, asking questions."

"Seattle?" Claudia asked, startled. "Did your stepuncle have relatives there?"

Janet shook her head. "There's no one but my mother and me. The manager said the two investigators presented cards from a company called Underground Investigations. He had them wait while he called both their office and the Better Business folks in their area. They checked out as far as he went."

"So what in the world did they want?"

"It seems they were interested in talking to the people who supposedly saw Albert get lifted into the air. And get this," Janet said, leaning forward as if to tell Claudia something really private. "They wanted to get a very recent picture of Albert."

"Picture?" Claudia asked. "If they were investigating his disappearance for someone, wouldn't they already know what he looked like?"

Janet shrugged and took a sip of her coffee. "It would seem that way to me."

"Weird," Claudia said.

"That it is," Janet said. "Tell McCallum. I've warned the manager of the rest home that McCallum's coming by."

"He said he'd do it as soon as he got back this afternoon from Idaho."

"Idaho?" Janet asked. "What's he doing in Idaho?"

Claudia frowned. "He never tells me about his cases, which I guess is a good thing."

Janet laughed. "That it is."

"But he did say it was another missing persons case that he had to check some facts on."

Janet nodded, then mumbled, "Tina Harris. Let's hope this case doesn't get that much press."

Claudia could only nod in agreement as it suddenly dawned on her what case McCallum was working on besides Janet's.

11

A mystery is something dark in itself which sheds light on everything around it.

—TIMOTHY HOLME
FROM *THE ASSISI MURDERS*

4:20 P.M. JUNE 23.
PORTLAND, OREGON

McCallum had spent the hour flight in the Harris corporate jet going back over the reports about the case more carefully than he had done the first time. He reread the four pages from the Search and Rescue, then the state police report, and the sheriff's added notes. Finally he reread the initial background check on Tina's boyfriend and on his family.

Nothing.

Usually he could see a place to start digging, or as Henry, his old doughnut-eating partner used to say, some string to pull that would start the entire mess unraveling. But with this case there was no obvious string and no "X" marking a good place to dig. At least so far.

But there had to be something. He scanned through the reports checking off possibilities.

One: Those kids hadn't walked out of that valley. Of that much he was fairly certain after seeing the area. They would have been spotted, since their camp was discovered so quickly.

Two: If they had drowned in the river, their bodies should have been found by now, what with all the rafters going down it every day and the low water level.

Three: There was zero sign of struggle in the camp, so however, or for whatever reason, they had left quickly. Either by raft or by air. And if they'd have been taken down the river by raft, they would have been spotted at the take-out point.

The only conclusion that McCallum could come to was that those kids were airlifted out of that valley. But taken to where?

By whom?

And for what reason?

There was no hint in the background of either teenager that they would do this purposefully, to run away from family.

The entire thing was starting to give McCallum a throbbing headache.

He gave Arthur all the files and told the kid to put them on his desk back at the office. Then he also told his youngest investigator to write up a report about the case, with any theory he might have, no matter how far-fetched. Maybe a young imagination could come up with something he had missed.

McCallum swung by his apartment, took a quick shower, and changed clothes. He desperately wanted to just turn the air conditioner up to high, lie down on the bed, and sleep until the following morning. That nap on the plane earlier in the day just hadn't been long enough, and the heat in the mountains had drained him. But he forced himself out the door and by a few minutes before five was pulling into the parking lot of North Hills Rest Home.

The place was a fairly nice-looking brick building surrounded by pine trees and flowering bushes. But inside it was nothing more than a standard nursing home, with stained tile floors, metal bars on the walls, and residents' pictures on the bulletin board.

As McCallum moved down the hall he remembered why he hated nursing homes so much. The smell. They always smelled like a cross between too much disinfectant and rotting human flesh. This one was no different, and the smell smothered him as he approached the main desk. He knew he was eventually going to have to take another shower to get it off.

The manager of the rest home turned out to be a sixty-year-old man by the name of Craig Wade. He wore a button-down yellow golf sweater and his tan slacks were stained with what looked like might have been someone's lunch a few days earlier.

Wade instantly recognized McCallum's name and escorted him into a small, cluttered, and very hot little office behind one of the nurses' stations.

And closed the door.

McCallum watched the wooden door close as though it was a cell door closing on death row. He wanted to scream, *Leave that open!* but instead just sat down.

After spending half the day in the Idaho wilderness's dry sun and heat, the last thing McCallum needed was to be trapped in a hot little office filled with the cloying smell of clean death.

"I'm here about the disappearance of Albert Hancer," McCallum said quickly, hoping to get this over with.

Wade nodded as he sat down across the desk from McCallum. "I know. The mayor told me this morning that I should open all my files to you about Albert. Anything I can do to help. Anything at all. Please just ask."

McCallum wanted to say, *Start by opening the damn door*. But he didn't. Instead he said, "Good. I appreciate that. First I'd like to talk to those who last saw Mr. Hancer."

Anything to get out of this hot office, but he didn't say that, either.

"You don't really believe," Wade said, leaning forward and whispering as if his office was bugged, "that Albert was abducted by aliens, do you?"

McCallum laughed. "I've seen a lot of strange things during my years on the force and working as an investigator. And not once have I seen an alien from space."

"Good," Wade said, acting relieved. "Those investigators this morning seemed to think he was. And I just can't have that getting out about North Hills Rest Home. It wouldn't be good for business, you know."

McCallum was about to ask Wade just exactly what *would* be good for business, when the fact that other investigators had already been here hit him. "Investigators from the police?"

Wade shook his head. "No. They were from Seattle. Here, I've got their card. I made a few calls before I talked to them, and they seemed to check out."

He shuffled the pile on the top of his desk for a moment and miraculously came up with a small business card, which he handed to McCallum. It was a simple brown card with the words "Underground Investigations" printed in block letters across the top. Two names were underneath, along with a Seattle address and phone number. McCallum didn't recognize either name, but that didn't mean anything.

"Why did you say they believed Mr. Hancer was abducted by aliens?"

"They came right out and said so," Wade said. "And all their questions were about that aspect of Albert's disappearance. They didn't even know what Albert looked like. Had to ask me for a picture."

The heat was slowly turning McCallum into a melting puddle. He had to get out of this office or they were going to have to carry him out. He stood. "Can I keep this card?"

Wade stood also. "Sure. I don't see why not."

"Good," McCallum said, stuffing the card in his pocket. "Now, if you'd be so kind, would you show me where Albert was last seen?"

"Be glad to," Wade said. "Any excuse to get out of this damn hot office."

McCallum managed not to laugh as Wade intently went around his cluttered desk and opened the door. The cool air over McCallum's face sent drops of water down his forehead and neck. Not only was he going to have to take a shower to get the nursing home smell off, now he needed another one in general.

Wade led the way down a wide hallway with doors opened on either side. All the rooms were lived in, but empty.

"Everyone's at dinner at the moment," Wade said by way of explanation.

Wade opened the door into an enclosed courtyard, completely closed in on all four sides by the nursing home. It was open to the air, and three large pine trees shaded half the courtyard from the evening sun. Two concrete paths led from double doors on two sides of the courtyard into a central patio area. Benches were scattered around the patio, all facing inward.

McCallum had a sinking feeling as the manager of the rest home stopped and pointed at a bench on the edge of the center patio. "He was sitting there."

"And I assume no one was with him?" McCallum asked, glancing around at the only two entrances into the courtyard. One was from the hall they had just come in from. The other led into a large room full of elderly people eating.

"No, actually there were three other residents out here," Wade said. "On hot summer evenings this is a favorite place for many. You can talk to them if you want, but you won't get much out of Mrs. Hillary. She hasn't been with us mentally for some time."

"Thanks," McCallum said. "So you're telling me that one minute he was sitting there and the next he was gone, huh?"

"Well," Wade said, his voice very hesitant. "This is where it gets sort of . . . well, odd." He cleared his throat and went on without looking at McCallum. "Albert was sitting on that bench. The head RN on swing shift, a wonderful woman named Tamara Wilson, was working meds in the south hall, right behind us."

Wade pointed at the door they had just come through, then went on. "She was standing at the med cart near that door. When she saw the white light she looked outside."

McCallum remembered from the police report that Claudia had given him that there had been a white light that had lifted Albert Hancer into the sky above the pine trees.

"The report said two of your staff saw Mr. Hancer disappear."

Wade nodded. "One of our cooks, a Mrs. Petty, was busing tables in the dinning room. She also saw the light and saw Albert get lifted into the air."

Now McCallum had a headache for certain. He walked to the bench where Albert Hancer had sat, then looked around. There was a clear field of vision from both doors. And no other way out of this area.

Yet Albert Hancer was missing.

Just like Tina Harris.

McCallum tried to shake the thought of the two cases being similar, but couldn't. Two impossible disappearances. One out of a walled mountain valley. Another out of a walled courtyard.

One in the middle of nowhere. The other in front of witnesses.

Both impossible on the surface.

He glanced around the courtyard one more time and the words *locked room* popped into his head. Of course. Both these cases were like locked-room mysteries. He'd read enough of those over the years to know that a simple explanation was always the way it turned out.

Always.

But McCallum wasn't sure he was going to like the explanation when he found it.

12

The less you understand the greater your faith.

—R. A. J. WALLING
FROM *WHY DID TRETHEWY DIE*

5:50 A.M. JUNE 24.
LOCATION UNKNOWN

Tina Harris managed to force open her crusty, dirt-filled eyes. The aliens had knocked them all out again, most likely to take someone to experiment on. A faint memory surfaced of Jerry lying on a table with his stomach cut open and she forced it away. It was clear to her that she had been taken for experiments. But until they came for her she didn't have to think about it.

Light was starting to come through the crack in the cave roof. Another day was about to start. She wasn't sure she could make it through the coming heat without more water. In five days in the cave she'd managed to get a few handfuls of grain-like food each day and a few small bottles of water that the aliens had left beside the door for them. The grain seemed to have been intended for cattle feed and the bottled water every day was clearly stolen off a truck. The aliens must have felt that their prisoners never deserved anything from the alien ship, but only stuff stolen from other humans. Even though the cattle feed and bottled water was left every day so far, it had been nowhere near enough to make it through the stifling heat that filled this cave in the afternoon. It was as if she were lying in an oven.

Around her she noticed that the aliens had removed some of the dead, but left others. It was as if they didn't really care what happened to those they had taken prisoner. And that made no sense to Tina. Why bother to kidnap humans if the aliens were only going to let them die?

Tina sat up slowly, doing her best to ignore the intense empty pain from her stomach. If she was going to get any food, going to survive another day, she had to move.

Around her a few others were slowly climbing to their feet and making their way toward the blocked mouth of the cave. They all looked like dirty, naked ghosts in the faint light.

She used a nearby rock to push herself to her feet and followed the others. After five days she was no longer bothered by being naked. Staying alive was much, much more important.

Near the door the aliens had left the same metal tub of some grain-like food. It looked like it was the same cattle feed. It would taste flat and stale, but it was at least food. She wondered what some poor farmer was thinking about his missing grain.

Two cases of human-made bottled water. Spring water in blue bottles with labels saying it was from somewhere in California. The aliens must have stolen the water from some truck or store. She didn't know why they just didn't give them water in buckets, but at that moment she didn't much care.

With the others, she tore into the cases and grabbed a bottle. She drank a good quarter of a bottle before taking a breath. She couldn't remember ever tasting anything so wonderful. And it was even somewhat cold. All the other mornings the bottled water had been warm.

Today it was like tasting heaven.

She squirted a little on her face and eyes, clearing out the dirt caked on over the last five days. She didn't have anything to wipe off the water, but she didn't care. It just felt wonderful.

She forced herself to take another, slower drink, then a handful of grain. Then more water.

Around her others were doing the same.

She took a large mouthful of grain, then took two full bottles of water and another handful of grain and moved back to the edge of the cave away from the door. Just maybe a few of them would now live another day or two.

What for, she didn't know.

Again the image of Jerry cut open on that alien table flashed in her mind and she knew the reason.

13

Reason is the method by which those who do not know the truth, step by step, finally discover it.

—MELVILLE DAVISSON POST
FROM *THE STRAW MAN*

7:03 A.M. JUNE 24.
BELLINGHAM, WASHINGTON

The statues of the two Klar towered over Neda Foster as she glanced up at the two men sitting in front of her desk. One of them was her chief investigator, Luke Ellis, who had returned last night from Portland. She had just finished reading his report on the abduction of Albert Hancer. There was nothing wrong with the report, but the contents bothered her. And those contents bothered her a lot.

The Klar were changing their patterns and habits. And that was not a good sign.

She turned to Dr. Cornell, a bald-headed man sitting to her right in a large, overstuffed chair. He looked fifty, but was actually barely forty. He had an overly-large nose, bad teeth, and held five different doctorate degrees. Cornell was her right hand, closest adviser, and chief researcher into alien actions. He had also witnessed the abduction of a close college friend twenty-one years ago and had put all his energies into researching the aliens ever since. If it wasn't for Cornell, Neda's program would not be as advanced as it was.

Yet at the moment it seemed as if they knew nothing.

Things were changing. The Klar, after almost fifty years, were changing patterns and habits. Now there was something happening with human abductions and it wasn't expected. And the oddest thing was that the Klar were taking the elderly out of nursing homes, and no one could come up with even a far-fetched reason why.

"How many does that make, Cornell?" Neda asked.

He didn't even need to look at the printout on his lap. "It seems they've abducted at least one elderly person near almost every major city around the world over the last week."

"Are any of the others this blatant?" Neda asked, tapping the Portland report. "With this many witnesses?"

Cornell nodded. "Over the last few days they're acting as if they don't much care who sees them. Not like their practices over the last fifty years. It's as if the end is almost here as far as they're concerned."

Neda nodded and Luke visibly paled, glancing up at the two looming statues and then back at Cornell. "You're kidding, right Doc?"

Cornell shook his head no.

"I've been thinking the same thing," Neda said. "But what do we do to stop them?"

"I don't think there is any stopping them," Cornell said. "We still don't know what they're planning, let alone where. Forget the minor problem of how to stop it."

"Well," Neda said, "it seems we'd better be finding out what they're up to first, huh?"

Cornell laughed. "Yeah, it would seem to be the next logical step."

After a moment of silence he continued, "It is also logical that if they're taking one elderly person from each city, they plan on using that person in that city."

Neda nodded. "A decent assumption. But for what reason? And much more importantly, how and when?"

Cornell shrugged. "We've studied the aliens for a long time. For a moment let's stay inside the information we already have. We've ascertained, from computer programs run with the information from fifty years of sighting, that the aliens have less than twenty ships worldwide."

Neda sighed, her stomach twisting even more than it had been. "Agreed. Go on."

"We'll assume," Cornell said, "no more ships are coming for now. If the reason they're becoming more bold is because more of their ships are arriving, we have no hope anyhow. So we'll go on and just skip that possibility."

Now Luke was really pale. He obviously hadn't thought of that possibility. Neda had, but like Cornell she figured that was best ignored.

Cornell continued. "We have assumed that they have a use for humans, beyond studying us. Most likely slave labor."

Neda hoped Cornell would get to his point soon. "So they now have use for an elderly person in every major city," Neda said. "We're back to how and why."

Cornell nodded. "My point exactly. Assuming that they have finally figured out a way to control humans, just to the why of it. What purpose would the aliens use an elderly person for in *every* city?"

Luke shrugged. "The cities are full of the elderly poor. Living in rooms and on the streets."

Cornell pointed to him, his face lighting up. "So they would fit in. Right?"

Luke nodded. "Yeah. Easily. No one would pay the slightest attention to another elderly person."

Neda leaned forward. "So what would the Klar want with the elderly in the cities? I'm just not following. Even if they could control them, to what use would an old person be put?"

Luke said softly, "Smuggling."

"What?" Neda asked.

"Oh, my, yes," Cornell said. "Of course."

"Well," Neda said, facing Luke. "Explain it to me. I must have missed a cup of coffee this morning."

"I worked in customs at Sea-Tac International for a year," Luke said. "We were constantly reminded by our bosses not to ignore elderly travelers as potential smugglers. Yet I found myself looking at a woman the age of my grandmother and not believing that a person that age could do anything wrong."

Suddenly the possibilities were starting to dawn on Neda. The Klar couldn't really fly their ships anywhere near the heart of a city without a high risk of being spotted. In all the years of abductions, the Klar had never taken people from the heart of cities. Never. The Klar had always acted as if they were afraid of the cities. So if they wanted something taken *into* a city, they had to have a human do it. That would be normal Klar thinking.

She turned to Cornell. "You said *every* major city?"

"Almost," Cornell said. "And we may have missed a few reports."

Neda turned to Luke. "How do we find them if they are in every city? How do we prove this is happening?"

"Start small," Luke said. "That's the theory of searches. Start small and expand the search pattern."

"Portland," Neda said, glancing at Cornell.

"Portland," he said, smiling.

She turned back to Luke. "We have to find out what those elderly people are doing and find out now! I want every person you can find, or hire, searching the streets of Portland with pictures of this Albert Hancer. Portland's a small enough city that we should be able to cover it. Find him if he's there."

Luke stood and without another word headed for the door. Neda knew he was good. And within a few hours she knew he'd have at least a hundred people on Portland's streets.

But for some reason that didn't feel like enough.

After he was gone Neda turned to Cornell. "Seems like a good day to take some of the staff and visit beautiful downtown Portland, doesn't it?"

He smiled. "I'll round up about twenty of my people and meet you at the airport hangar in twenty minutes."

"I'll match your twenty," she said as he headed for the door.

She waited for the door to close, then picked up the phone and dialed a very private number she'd only been given the day before. The vice president needed to know what they were doing. And he just might be able to round up a little help himself.

14

The reading of detective stories is simply a kind of vice that, for silliness and minor harmfulness, ranks somewhere between crossword puzzles and smoking.

—EDMUND WILSON
FROM AN ARTICLE IN *THE NEW YORKER*

1:15 P.M. JUNE 24.
PORTLAND, OREGON

Frustrating described McCallum's morning.

He had spent two hours going over every detail about Tina Harris's disappearance, from the photos of the camp to the reports on her boyfriend's father. Nothing to give him even the slightest clue. At eleven he had called a staff meeting and all four of his hired detectives brainstormed over the case. The kid with the freckles, Arthur, came up with the same theory McCallum had: the kids were flown out of that valley. But he had no reason why, either.

So after almost two hours of meetings he had the same result he started the morning with: Nothing.

So by one he was hungry, tired, and frustrated. He called Henry, hoping his ex-partner hadn't eaten yet. As it turned out, due to a bank robbery right before lunch, Henry hadn't. And he wasn't happy about the fact.

They met at a little deli called Joe's on Burnside, across from Powell's Bookstore. The place was small, but it had great chowder and sandwiches. Henry hated the booths there because his stomach was almost too large for him to get into them, but the food was good enough to overcome that one minor problem.

Henry spent the first part of the lunch harping on the stupidity of banks and their alarm systems and swearing he was going to quit the force and start that doughnut shop. Then finally, halfway through a large tuna sandwich, he asked McCallum about the Idaho trip.

McCallum told him his frustrations and lack of progress, and laid out what he had seen and read. Henry had no suggestions. He said it was just plain weird.

"Yeah, weird is right," McCallum said, agreeing. "But not as strange as the Hancer disappearance up on the north side."

Over the last bite of his tuna sandwich Henry looked at McCallum. "You working on that case, too?"

McCallum nodded. "Afraid so."

"Sure is nice you can afford to hire so much help," Henry said, shoving his plate to the edge of the table.

"Help?" McCallum asked. "I just got the four, and Arthur is so damn young I don't know what to do with him half the time."

"So then, who do you have working the streets?" Henry asked. "We got a call this morning saying the family was going to show some pictures around downtown today to see if they could find him. Last I heard there were a dozen or so at least. Damned if I know what they're going to find, but I suppose it couldn't hurt."

"Family?" McCallum asked. He was getting more and more confused by the moment. From the file he'd gotten on Albert Hancer, the only family the guy had was the mayor's mother. He never had kids and the mayor was an only child.

Henry finished his Coke and waved for the waitress. "Lemon pie," he shouted when he got her attention.

McCallum glanced at his watch. It was approaching two in the afternoon. Claudia would be in the office. He shoved the uneaten part of his ham sandwich away and told Henry he'd be right back. He went to the front desk and borrowed their phone, cussing at himself for not making time to get a cell phone. One of these days he'd do it. It was the nineties thing to do.

It took him only a moment before he confirmed with Claudia exactly what he had thought: No family of Albert Hancer had paid for a search for him. He had no family to do so.

Henry was about halfway through his lemon pie when McCallum slid back into place across from him. "No family," McCallum said. "I'm the only one hired on the Hancer case. But yesterday two guys from Seattle were asking questions at the nursing home."

Henry gave McCallum a puzzled look. "Then who has all the manpower out there on the streets?"

McCallum only shrugged, smiling at the puzzled look on his ex-partner's face.

"Damn," Henry said. "If it's not the stupid banks, it's something else." He popped one more large forkful of pie into his mouth, then pointed at the check as he worked his stomach out of the booth. "You're buying."

15

You can't have a tin can tied to your tail and go through life pretending it isn't there.

—JOSEPHINE TEY
FROM *THE FRANCHISE AFFAIR*

1:30 P.M. JUNE 24.
SAN FRANCISCO, CALIFORNIA

The vice president of the United States walked off the luncheon dais after his speech to a local San Francisco women's group and moved purposefully up to Louise, his top aide. She was in her mid-fifties and was known inside the Beltway as one of the top political strategists in the business. She was also fiercely loyal to Alan Wallace and everyone knew she'd run his presidential campaign when the time came. And most likely end up as chief of staff if he won.

"Let's go," he said to her and, with two Secret Service men behind them, they moved quickly through the back door and into the waiting limo.

After they were both in and alone, and the limo was

headed for the airport he turned to her. "Any word yet from Portland?"

"Nothing," she said. "I checked just before you finished your speech and they had found nothing so far." She reached into her briefcase and pulled out a file. "Here's all the material you asked for. Had to call in a favor to get it this fast."

He nodded and opened the file. It didn't take him long to confirm from the documents in front of him that elderly people had gone missing over the last week in almost every major city of the world. Ten of the reports had credible witnesses saying that the abductees were lifted into the air by a white light. Neda Foster had been right. The vision of those statues of the Klar standing over him made him feel cold. He'd had nightmares last night thinking about real Klar standing over him.

He looked up at Louise and indicated the report. "Did you read this?"

She nodded.

"What do you think?"

"To be honest," she said, "it gives me the creeps."

The vice president nodded. "You should have seen those two statues they have. Hollywood couldn't have done it better."

"No thanks," Louise said. "I have enough trouble sleeping at night worrying about your speeches. I don't need aliens, too."

They rode in silence for a moment. Then he closed the file. "What am I going to do with this?" He tapped the manila file on his leg.

"I assume that's a real question," Louise said.

The vice president smiled. "It is. To be honest, I don't really know what I should be doing."

"My suggestion," Louise said, "is wait. You've sent what help you can. See what they find in Portland. That's what Neda recommended also, wasn't it?"

The vice president nodded. "If the aliens do exist. And if they are planting something in the cities using the elderly, I just hope we don't wait too long."

Louise took the file from his hands and put it back into her briefcase.

"Damn," the vice president said. "Why, of all the people in the government, did Neda and her father pick me to tell?"

Louise gave him no answer and they rode the rest of the way to the airport in silence.

16

A realist is somebody who thinks the world is simple enough to be understood. It isn't.

—DONALD WESTLAKE
FROM AN ARTICLE IN *MURDER INK*

1:40 P.M. JUNE 24.
PORTLAND, OREGON

Using Henry's car, they cruised the streets along Burnside near the river. Henry and McCallum hadn't cruised the streets in a car, just looking, since the days of their first patrols. McCallum clearly didn't miss it, especially since Henry's air-conditioning was out.

Finally, about the point McCallum was going to melt right into the front seat, he spotted a group of five men in suits standing on a corner. One of the men looked as if he was holding an eight-by-ten photo in one hand. Amid the old buildings in this area, McCallum had never seen a group who looked so much out of place as those guys.

"Bingo," Henry said when McCallum pointed them out. He pulled over beside them and shut off the car. "Let me do the talking," he said to McCallum as he pushed open his door.

McCallum didn't much care who did the talking. He just wanted a few answers. And after all the questions and frustrations of the last few days, and the heat of Henry's car, just about any answer would do. He was in *that* kind of mood.

McCallum climbed out as Henry moved around the front of the car and flashed his badge at the men. "Portland PD," he said. "You fellows looking for Albert Hancer?"

One of the men, a tall guy with red hair and freckles around his eyes, stepped forward. "Yes, we are, sir," he said.

McCallum noted that the others sort of dropped back behind the redhead. They were clearly a group of men used to working together and the redhead was without doubt in charge.

"Having any luck?" Henry asked, doing his friendly act. McCallum had seen him do it hundreds of times, and most of the time it got the answers they needed. It had also gotten Henry punched a few times, too.

"I'm afraid not," the redhead said. "We were about to spread out and try this street here." He pointed down past three of the city's older hotels that stood side by side along the right. All three dated from the turn of the century and were rattraps used by the poor, the elderly, and streetwalkers.

"Too bad," Henry said. Then he glanced down the street before turning back to the redhead. "Who exactly are you guys working for?"

The redhead reached into his breast pocket and pulled out a brown card as if he'd been doing it all day. And most likely had.

Henry studied the card and then handed it to McCallum. It had the same name—Underground Investigations—as the card of the two men who had talked to the nursing home manager. Only this card had no name on it.

McCallum raised an eyebrow as he handed it back to Henry, letting Henry know he'd seen the card before, but wouldn't say where at the moment.

Henry turned back to the redhead. "Mind if I talk to your boss? My lieutenant wants me to make periodic checks on your progress, since it's an open case on our books and we're kind of hoping you find the guy."

The redhead nodded. He reached inside his jacket and plucked a cell phone off his belt. With a quick punch of numbers and a short wait he said, "Sir, I have a police detective here who's checking into our progress for his department. He'd like to talk to you."

McCallum watched as the redhead nodded to whatever words his boss was saying, then clicked off the phone and replaced it. "They're two blocks to the north of here," he said to Henry. "He'll be waiting on the north corner with three others."

"Thanks," Henry said. "And good hunting."

All five men smiled at them as they climbed back into the now even hotter interior of Henry's car. McCallum could tell the smiles were very nervous, as if they were hiding something. But he had no idea what it might be.

"This is just too damn strange," Henry said. "Never seen anything quite like it before."

McCallum totally agreed with Henry. He'd never even heard of anything like this happening before. "You notice they were all carrying?" McCallum asked.

Henry nodded. "Yeah. Hope they're not planning on gunning down the old guy when they find him."

McCallum only snorted at Henry's attempt at humor as Henry made a wide U-turn and headed north, going just fast enough to cool McCallum a few degrees.

A block later Henry nodded toward a group of five more suited men walking up the sidewalk on the right carrying photos. They, too, were clearly out of place in this area of town.

"So why," McCallum said, "would a small army of armed men spend a day in Portland searching for an elderly man no one cared about when he wasn't missing?"

"That's something I intend to find out," Henry said.

McCallum certainly hoped so. The more this case and the Harris case progressed, the more questions he had. In all his years he'd never had anything like this happen before. Usually questions led to answers.

All these questions led to was more questions.

"So you've never read of anything like this in one of those mysteries of yours?" Henry asked.

"If I had," McCallum said, "would I be roasting my tail out here on the streets with you?"

"A fella can hope," Henry said as he pulled over into an open space a half block short of the designated corner. Within a half minute they were crossing the street toward a group of four waiting on the corner in the shade of the building.

Three men and a woman stood and watched them approach. McCallum could tell that two of the men were like the others, professionals carrying weapons; most likely licensed revolvers in shoulder holsters under their arms. The other man was a computer-nerd looking guy, balding and wearing an old T-shirt. The woman was a tall, statuesque blonde wearing a silk blouse and designer pants. She appeared to be in her thirties and she was still turning the heads of those walking by on the sidewalk.

Henry, with McCallum following, walked up to them with his badge held in front of him so they could all see it.

The woman stepped forward, smiling first at Henry, then a little more friendlily at McCallum. "Glad your department is checking on our progress, Detective," she said. "I'm Neda Foster." She pointed to the nerdy guy. "This is Dr. Cornell."

Dr. Cornell smiled at Henry and then at McCallum, but McCallum could tell the doctor was clearly nervous for some reason. Maybe the same reason the other guys down the street were nervous.

Neda went on with her quick introductions. "This is Lyle Wilson, head of Underground Investigations of Seattle."

McCallum knew the name from the card. Same guy who had gone to the nursing home.

Neda then indicated the second man, wearing a fairly expensive suit and a dress hat that shielded his face from the sun. "This is Robert Earhart of the FBI."

McCallum wasn't sure, but he thought he saw Neda Foster almost break out laughing at the looks that must have been on both his and Henry's faces. Robert Earhart was not only *with* the FBI, he was the director of the western division of the FBI.

Earhart stepped forward and extended his hand to Henry. "Glad to meet you, Detective . . . ?"

"Greer," Henry managed to say as he shook the FBI director's hand.

Then Earhart turned to McCallum. "I didn't catch your name?" he said, extending his hand.

"Richard McCallum, of McCallum Investigations. I was hired by the family to find Albert Hancer."

Neda Foster's face turned into a stone mask and McCallum had a hard time not smiling right back at her as he shook Earhart's hand.

"Well," Earhart said, stepping back beside Neda Foster, "it seems we all have an interest in finding Albert Hancer."

"Some more than others," Henry said. "Just how many people do you have working this search?"

Neda laughed. "Enough to find Albert Hancer, we hope."

There was a faint chime and Earhart said, "Excuse me." He pulled out a small phone from his jacket pocket and clicked it open. Without a word of hello he simply listened, then said, "I'll meet him there." Then he clicked the phone closed.

He turned halfway to Neda Foster, but without any thought of keeping his information from McCallum or Henry, he said, "The vice president has altered his schedule and is flying here. I'll meet him at the airport."

Neda nodded.

Without another word Earhart turned to Henry and said, "Nice meeting you, Detective." Then nodded to McCallum. "Mr. McCallum."

Then he turned and strode up the street.

"*The* vice president?" Henry said softly as he looked at McCallum. "Is *he* looking for this guy, too?"

McCallum turned to Neda Foster. "Is he, Ms. Foster?"

Neda Foster laughed, a simple laugh that seemed to hang in the air between her and McCallum. Then, with a smile that said clearly that she was enjoying toying with McCallum, she said, "Yes. Actually he is."

"McCallum," Henry said, his voice half angry. "What have you gotten me into?"

"That," McCallum said, "is a question I hope Ms. Foster can answer."

She smiled at him. "I hope so, too."

17

A hole in the ice is dangerous only to those who go skating.

—REX STOUT
FROM *TOO MANY COOKS*

2:10 P.M. JUNE 24.
NEAR HELLS CANYON AREA, OREGON

The hot sun beat down on the two men in the open Jeep as they bounced over rocks and sagebrush on a road that seemed to have given up the claim to the name years before. Now only two faint tracks through the brush led the way. The rolling, sagebrush-covered hills of the high Oregon desert seemed to stretch into infinity on three sides, with sharp, snowcapped mountain peaks blocking the way in front. Hells Canyon, the world's deepest gorge, ran down the middle of those mountains, forming the border between Oregon and Idaho.

Cobb Turner drove his new Jeep Cherokee, his black hair streaming behind him as he laughingly forced the Jeep forward, bouncing over anything that got in his way. Cobb's father owned a twelve thousand acre cattle ranch to the west of their location. Cobb had been born and raised on that ranch, and had come home for the summer from his second year at the University of California at Berkeley. As far as he was concerned this area was his personal backyard and he loved it here. He didn't notice the heat, his suntanned body covered only with cut-off Levis.

Beside him, clearly not enjoying himself half as much as Cobb was J. W. Steele. Steele had been Cobb's roommate in Berkeley and had agreed to come to the eastern Oregon ranch to see him for a few weeks. Fair-skinned and originally from the midwest, the dry heat of the high desert had been keeping him inside the big house at the ranch more than anywhere. Today, to protect himself from the burning heat, Steele wore a long-sleeved cotton shirt, Levis, and a wide-brimmed hat. With one hand he gripped the dashboard while holding his hat in place over the bumps with the other.

"Almost there," Cobb shouted over the roar of the engine as they bounced over another ridge and went into a dust-swirling descent into a small gully. He banged the jeep through a wash and then shifted down to spin dirt out behind him as they fishtailed up the bank on the other side.

Cresting the top opened up a wide vista of hot high-desert country. In front of them a steep, rock-walled canyon twisted off in both directions. A stream twisted its way through the middle of the canyon two hundred feet below, surrounded by green bushes and small trees. It was the only green as far as the eye could see.

The canyon was called Sheepeater Canyon after a family who had homesteaded it a hundred years ago and then had to kill mountain goats to get enough food to live through a hard winter. They had left the following spring and no one had lived near the canyon for over a hundred years. Their old homestead was now nothing more than a pile of logs near the north end of the canyon.

During the first settlers' stay in the canyon they had discovered a series of caves, now called the Sheepeater Caves. They were large lava tubes that had been exposed to the air when the canyon was formed. As a kid, Cobb and his brothers had explored a lot of the caves. He hadn't been back for over ten years and finally, this summer, he was making the time.

Cobb wound the jeep along the top of the canyon for a half mile until the road finally dead-ended with rock cliffs falling away on both sides.

Within minutes Cobb was leading the way, headed down a steep rock-and-sand trail into the canyon with Steele doing his best not to fall. Both men carried flashlights, a bottle of water, and some snacks. Cobb figured they'd spend an hour or so in the main cave, then head back for dinner.

It took them a good twenty, very hot minutes to make their way down the two hundred foot wall of the canyon and another twenty minutes to work their way up the brush-covered canyon to the mouth of the main cave. Cobb couldn't remember it taking that long as a kid, but memory did that sometimes.

The mouth of the cave was huge, over one hundred feet from ground to top and double that wide. Cobb knew it got even larger inside. It was a spectacular natural room that early Indians in the region had used for shelter. He and his brothers had spent many a fun afternoon in that big cave.

"What do you think?" Cobb asked, pointing up at the huge opening in the side of the rock canyon wall.

"Wow," Steele said between pants. "That's big."

"Told you," Cobb said, scrambling up the slight incline to the mouth of the cave. "Watch for snakes."

"Snakes!" Steele said.

"Rattlers," Cobb said, without turning around. "They won't bother you unless you step on them. Just be careful."

Cobb crested the slight incline so he could see down into the cave and stopped. "What in hell is—" A white light shot out of the cave and caught him. After a moment he slumped to the ground.

From behind him Steele saw the white light catch his friend. "Cobb?" he shouted as his friend fell. That was the last word he got out of his mouth.

A large, snake-like being stepped up beside Cobb's body and aimed something at Steele. The white light froze Steele in position.

A moment later he, too, was unconscious.

The next morning Cobb's Jeep was found one hundred fifty miles to the west, parked at a popular swimming area in the Columbia Gorge. The men's clothes were piled on the backseat.

They were presumed drowned.

18

Facts are not judgments, and judgments are not facts.

—DICK FRANCIS
FROM *IN THE FRAME*

2:15 P.M. JUNE 24.
PORTLAND, OREGON

For the past twenty minutes McCallum had become more and more frustrated. And he had been pretty frustrated to begin with. After Earhart of the FBI left, Neda Foster had excused her group for a moment, without answering one of McCallum's questions. They had retreated to a spot near the brick building, in the shade. That's where the three of them had stayed, talking for the entire time while McCallum and Henry stood near the corner, doing their best to stay out of the hot sun.

Five minutes before, Henry had gone and gotten them both ice-filled lemonades from a nearby cafe. Those were now gone, as was McCallum's patience. He was about to barge in on their little conference when the guy from Underground Investigations plucked his cell phone out of his pocket. He quickly snapped it closed and the group headed for McCallum.

"There's been no luck finding him yet," the tall blonde said. "We're planning to continue searching for another hour and then call it off."

McCallum looked at Henry, then asked, "Got any other plans for the afternoon?"

Henry laughed. "None that really matter."

McCallum turned back to Neda Foster. He had a plan to get some answers out of them. "Let me get this straight, since you've given us no answers. You and your people are searching for Albert Hancer. Correct?"

Neda Foster nodded.

"And you think he may have checked into a room in this area sometime over the last week."

"Somewhere in the *center* of the city," Dr. Cornell said. "Where an elderly person would not be noticed. At least that's the theory we're working on."

McCallum heard the word center. These poorer neighborhoods were near the center, but not exactly at the center. "Well, there may be a few places you're missing. Places only locals like us would know."

Neda Foster looked at Cornell and her security man, then turned back to McCallum. "If you wouldn't mind helping us check them out, it would really help."

McCallum laughed. "As Henry said, we're not really that busy the next hour or so. But only if you promise to answer a few of my questions when we're finished."

"You have a deal, Mr. McCallum," Neda Foster said, sticking out her hand so they could shake on it.

McCallum took her firm hand and shook it, hoping his sweaty grasp wasn't bothering her too much. Then he turned to Henry. "The Sundown Hotel first, then maybe the old Radison."

Henry nodded. "We'll use my car."

With Henry driving, McCallum riding shotgun, and the other three in the backseat, they covered the fifteen blocks quickly. McCallum would have wagered anything that this was the first time that Neda Foster had ever been in the backseat of a police car.

The Sundown was an old turn-of-the-century hotel, five stories tall, situated in the center of a bunch of old warehouses now converted to stores and shops. It was one of those old hotels the city left standing to help take care of the housing problem. Mostly hotels like the Sundown were rat-infested dumps run by landlords who spent most of their time at the country club.

They all climbed out of the car and McCallum turned to Neda Foster. "Let me go in and ask. You got an extra picture?"

The investigator handed McCallum a picture of Albert Hancer taken a few months back in the nursing home. It had been blown up and the image cleaned up before it was reproduced. These people sure had the money and knew what they were doing.

Inside, the smell of age and stale piss hit McCallum. Two elderly men sat on two ancient overstuffed couches in what passed as a tiny lobby. An old television flickered in one corner, turned to a soap opera. The front desk was a cage, and a narrow wooden staircase climbed upward beside it. It was cooler in there than on the sidewalk outside, but not by much.

A guy in a T-shirt sat in the cage reading one of the tabloid papers. McCallum didn't recognize him, but that didn't mean that much after three years off the force. Or maybe the guy had never been in trouble with the law. McCallum figured anything was possible.

McCallum walked up and slid the picture through the cage. "I'm looking for a missing person. I'm working for the family."

The guy hardly glanced at the picture. "I don't pay much attention to who lives here. As long as they pay their rent on time every week. At the moment everyone's paid up."

McCallum pulled out his wallet, took a hundred dollar bill, and slid it on top of the picture. He made sure he kept his finger on the money until the guy picked up the picture and gave it a good look.

It was clear almost from the moment the guy actually looked at the picture that McCallum had hit pay dirt. Finally the guy took the bill and slid the picture back.

"Yeah. That old guy's been staying here. First room at the top of the stairs. Haven't seen him come or go in five days, though. For all I know he might be dead in there."

McCallum went back to the door and motioned for the others to come in. Then he went back to the desk. "Key?"

"I can't give out keys to just anyone who asks," the guy said.

"If the guy is dead, we may find a way to charge you for his death," McCallum said. "Right, Henry?"

Henry flipped open his badge. "Right on, partner."

The guy's face went white and he slid the key to McCallum.

"He's actually up there?" Neda Foster said.

"Shit!" Dr. Cornell said. "Shit! Shit! Shit!"

McCallum glanced at Cornell, actually shocked at the nerdy doctor's outburst. "I thought you wanted to find this guy."

Cornell just looked very worried, so McCallum shrugged

at Henry and led the way up the old wooden staircase. In the narrow hall at the top the stale smell of piss increased, as did the temperature. It had to be well over a hundred degrees in that hall and it was going to get hotter very fast.

Henry stopped in front of the door at the top of the stairs and waited until everyone was silent, then turned and knocked on the door. "Mr. Hancer? Police. I need to talk with you a moment. Open up."

No answer from inside.

Henry pounded again on the door, this time harder. "Mr. Hancer. It's the police. Please open the door."

Silence filled the crowded hall.

Henry drew his gun and said, "McCallum, you want to help me here?"

McCallum nodded and moved up beside Henry. Over the years as partners on the force they had gone through a lot of doors together. They knew the drill and they both trusted each other. McCallum only wished now that he had strapped on his gun. He didn't know why he'd need it against an elderly man, but he felt naked going through a door without it.

"Open it and I'll go through first," Henry said. "The rest of you move back down the hall a few steps."

They all did as they were told and McCallum stuck the key in the door and turned it, then quickly stepped away.

Henry pushed the door open with his foot and went in, ducking to the left.

McCallum, no gun in hand, scooted quickly in to the right.

The smell of rot caught McCallum in the face, choking him. Not the smell of a decomposed body. McCallum had smelled that a lot of times, more than he wanted to remember. This smell was an earthy, rotting smell that seemed to clog every inch of the air, choking off the oxygen.

"God!" Henry said, stopping and putting his hand over his nose. "What a smell."

McCallum stepped up beside Henry, doing everything he could to hold his stomach in place and stared at the scene in front of him.

Albert Hancer sat on the bed. Or at least something that looked like Albert Hancer. Hancer's body seemed to have started to slough off, as if his skin was dripping off his bones a layer at a time. Red blood dripped slowly from a dozen places on the guy, and his clothes were stained a rust red. McCallum swore that the guy looked as if he was melting.

But what startled McCallum the most was the fact that Albert Hancer was still breathing, and that his eyes were open, staring at a large suitcase on a cart sitting in the middle of the room.

McCallum tugged on Henry's shirt and pointed to the suitcase. "Let's not touch that."

"Understood," Henry said. He turned to those coming in the door. "Stay away from the suitcase!"

"Oh, shit!" Neda Foster's voice said behind McCallum. Then she yelled back through the door, "Cornell!"

"Someone call an ambulance," Henry shouted.

"No!" Neda Foster said. "Please. Not yet. I'll explain, but first let Dr. Cornell look at him. And I totally agree. No one should touch that suitcase." She turned to the man in charge of Underground Investigations, who had remained just outside the door. "Call for help. Seal off this building. No one is to come up here. Understood?"

McCallum saw him nod and head off down the hall as

Cornell slowly entered the room, his face white. McCallum could tell the doctor wasn't used to this sort of thing. McCallum had seen a lot of death and smelled a lot of human rot, but nothing like this before. Someone new would never be able to get near the source of that smell.

But somehow Cornell managed to keep his lunch down and moved very slowly over near the unmoving Albert Hancer.

McCallum watched him for a short moment, then turned to Neda Foster. "Maybe now it's time for some answers. What's in that suitcase?"

Ms. Foster swallowed, not taking her eyes off the suitcase. "Mr. McCallum," she said. "I don't really know. And that's the truth. I wish to God I did."

McCallum could actually see fear in Neda Foster's blue eyes. Without turning away from McCallum, she pulled out her cell phone and dialed a number. "This is Neda Foster. I need to talk to the vice president."

McCallum's stomach twisted and he stared at her for a moment, then turned and looked first at the awful mess of Albert Hancer, then at the suitcase. What in the hell was he in the middle of?

"Mr. Vice President," Neda Foster said. "We found him. And there's a suitcase with him."

"No!" Cornell half shouted. Then he said, "Shit! Shit! Shit!" really fast.

"Hold on, sir."

Everyone turned to Cornell as he rose from his knees beside Albert Hancer and wiped his hands on his pants. "Shit," Cornell said again. "It's not possible."

"What's not possible, Cornell?" Neda Foster asked.

"That's not possible," Cornell said, pointing at the sick

old man sitting on the bed, not moving. "It's just not possible."

"Cornell!" Neda Foster half-shouted. "Damn it! Would you explain what you mean?"

Cornell glanced at his boss and then back at the man sitting on the bed. "That's not human. I don't know what it is, exactly, but it's not human. It just looks human."

"Are you sure?" Neda Foster asked, taking in the wild words of Cornell as if she heard things like that every day.

McCallum, on the other hand, was having his troubles with what the doctor was saying. The guy was clearly a quack, plain and simple. And what the sick old guy on the bed needed was a fast trip to the hospital. And McCallum was thinking of hauling him there himself. But the suitcase stopped him. For some reason that suitcase scared McCallum, and he didn't know exactly why.

Cornell took a deep breath of the foul-smelling air and straightened his shoulders. "One of my degrees is medical, Neda. You know that. Of *course* I'm sure. That—*thing*—is not human and never was."

Neda Foster stared at the "thing" on the bed, then put the phone back to her ear. "Mr. Vice President, it's worse than we thought."

McCallum looked at Henry and Henry looked at him. Then both of them turned to look at the person on the bed that a doctor was saying really wasn't a person. For the first time in all their years working together, neither one of them had anything to say.

Not even anything funny.

19

The most commonplace incident takes on a new appearance if the attendant circumstances are unusual.

—MARY ROBERTS RINEHART
FROM *THE CIRCULAR STAIRCASE*

2:30 P.M. JUNE 24.
LOCATION UNKNOWN

For the first time, the aliens didn't bother to knock out the occupants of the prison as they opened the door.

At the moment the door opened Tina was sitting on the ground, leaning against a rock, trying to let the ground and the rock help her stay cool. She had hidden both her remaining bottles of water in a small hole between her naked body and the rock.

For the last few hours she had been playing a game with herself to slow down her desire to drink. She promised herself she could take a small taste of water every time she counted to five thousand. And if she missed count she had to start over. That way she would make her water last as long as possible and it kept her mind busy. But the heat of the afternoon already had the cave baking its occupants, and she wasn't sure how much longer she could go on, even with the water.

The heat was just too much.

The door made a high, screeching sound and then opened. At first Tina thought she was having hallucinations from the heat, then slowly realized it was real.

She had never once heard that door.

She turned, hoping beyond hope that someone had finally come to rescue them. A white light shone in and seemed to freeze everyone in place. Tina couldn't move, but she could still remember that same light from the night she was abducted. That seemed a lifetime ago.

It was a lifetime ago. The coolness of the mountain nights with Jerry. She could barely remember them, now.

This white light didn't make her body tingle as much as she remembered the first time.

There was a thump on the ground near the door. Then the white light vanished and the metal door ground shut, the final bang echoing like a signal of doom through the cave.

After the light vanished, Tina could move again. She took one bottle out from under her and sipped. Then she put it back and watched as someone near the door stood and went to check what the aliens had brought.

After a moment Tina heard a moan and someone sat up. They hadn't brought supplies. Only another prisoner, who would soon die with the rest of them, either from the heat or the aliens' experiments.

She took a shallow breath, curled against the faint coolness of the stone, and began her slow count, doing her best to ignore the heat.

20

Who makes the rules in this less than perfect world?

—B. M. GILL
FROM *VICTIMS*

2:35 P.M. JUNE 24.
PORTLAND, OREGON

It took only twelve minutes before the regional director of the FBI showed up in the hot, smelly room of Albert Hancer. Or what was posing as Albert Hancer.

But it was a long, hot, and smelly twelve minutes for McCallum. The entire time he kept debating if he and Henry should just take the old guy to the hospital. And each time, the sight of the old guy staring at the suitcase stopped McCallum from taking action.

During the waiting McCallum and Henry had moved back near the door and listened as Dr. Cornell talked with Neda Foster about the "thing-on-the-bed," as the doctor called it. He said that, the best he could tell, it was some sort of copy, like the latex masks actors used to change their looks.

But McCallum didn't buy that theory. And neither did Henry. This was an entire moving mask that seemed to breathe and never blinked as it stared at the suitcase in the middle of the room. Not hardly.

And, Cornell had said, the mask-thing-on-the-bed was falling apart, mostly due to the intense heat in the room. Albert Hancer's copy, in other words, was simply melting. Both Henry and McCallum had laughed when he proclaimed that.

McCallum believed in an old investigator's way of looking at the world: Occam's Razor principle, that the most logical and simple solution usually was the correct one. McCallum figured that Hancer had some sort of sickness that was causing his skin to have that melting look. And, as Henry said, "I hope that's not contagious." If it was, it was too late the moment they busted into the room.

The FBI director entered the heat and smell without even so much as a wrinkled nose, walked up to the thing-on-the-bed and gave it a once over. Then he walked around the suitcase, studying it. McCallum had to hand the guy one thing. He was cool. Very cool.

He motioned for McCallum and Henry to join him with Neda Foster and Dr. Cornell.

"I'm not sure that I buy the theory that the guy there isn't human," Director Earhart said.

"He's not," Dr. Cornell said.

Earhart went on, ignoring the doctor. "But he's clearly in strange shape. And the copy idea is the theory I've been ordered by the vice president to proceed under. At least until we know more about what's going on."

McCallum could tell he wasn't happy about his "orders" and most likely didn't know much more about what was going on here than McCallum or Henry did. McCallum wasn't sure if that made him feel better or worse.

"We're to take 'that' to your lab in Bellingham," Earhart said. "If he is human, he'll get medical attention there. And keep this quiet. Is that possible, Detective?"

Henry shrugged. "For the vice president I can keep it under wraps until you tell me otherwise."

McCallum looked at the director. "I'm afraid you might have another problem. The only family that man—" McCallum pointed at the bed. "—has is the mayor of this city. She hired me to find him. And since I did, I need to tell her something. I think the guy needs a hospital now and I won't even try to make this *copy* theory fly with the mayor. No chance."

"Shit," Neda Foster said.

"You still haven't found him," Cornell said. "That is just a copy of the original man. Nothing more."

"It still looks human to me, *Doctor*," McCallum said. "That guy might be really sick, but he's still a breathing human sitting there as far as I'm concerned."

"But he's not," Cornell said.

"Either way," McCallum said, turning back to Earhart, "the mayor is going to have to be told something and she knows you folks had the massive manhunt on down here today for her stepuncle. She wants to know why."

Earhart glanced at Neda, then back to McCallum. "The vice president and I can talk to the mayor."

McCallum smiled. "All right by me." Wait until Claudia sat through that meeting. Just the thought made McCallum smile.

"For now," Earhart said, "let's get whatever or whoever *that* is out of here. There's an ambulance waiting outside."

"I don't think it's going to be that simple," Neda said. She pointed to the suitcase. "There may be a connection between the suitcase and the thing-on-the-bed."

Earhart nodded. "John!"

There was movement in the hall and two men in suits carrying cases entered the room. Both of them were stopped short by the smell and both their faces went white at the sight of Albert Hancer on the bed.

"Check that suitcase," Earhart said. "Any outside links, especially with the guy on the bed."

Everyone in the room watched as they expertly set up the two equipment cases on either side of Albert Hancer's suitcase and went to work. Only the faint sounds of cars on the street broke the silence in the room as they worked. After a few minutes the one closest to them said, "Shit!"

"Favorite term with this group," Henry whispered to McCallum.

"Yeah," McCallum whispered back. "Seems that way."

"What is it?" Earhart asked, stepping forward.

The guy looked up. "Sir, there's no link from that to anything outside. At least at the moment. But sir, that's a bomb."

"Shit," Henry said.

McCallum agreed totally.

"What kind of bomb?" Earhart asked. "Can you tell?"

The other man looked up, fear in his eyes.

That was a look McCallum had always hoped he would never see on the face of a bomb squad man.

"Sir, it appears to be some sort of remote-controlled hydrogen bomb."

"Hydrogen bomb!" Henry said. "You're kidding?"

"You are certain?" Earhart said. "Is it armed? Does it have any motion sensors on it?"

"It's armed, sir," the man with fear in his eyes said.

The other studied his instruments. "No motion detectors, sir. Some sort of remote control hooked to it, though."

"They're not kidding," McCallum said softly to Henry. Over the years McCallum had been around his share of bombs, but never one that could level the entire city of Portland. Just the thought of it numbed him.

"I was afraid of that," Neda Foster said, softly.

It took a moment for McCallum to fully understand that the hot, foul-smelling little hotel room he was in was at ground zero of a hydrogen bomb.

And a moment longer still to realize that Neda Foster had feared this might happen.

21

You can't help stepping on everyone else's toes when you're all dancing around the golden calf.

—JAN EKSTROM
FROM *DEADLY REUNION*

2:50 P.M. JUNE 24.
PORTLAND, OREGON

Claudia hadn't gotten much work done all afternoon. After McCallum's phone call earlier, about all the men searching for Albert Hancer, she and the mayor had spent two hours making phone calls and trying to figure out who in Albert's past would do such a thing. They came up with a big fat zero. There just wasn't anyone. So after a late lunch they both tried to go back to work, but very little was coming from it.

Then Claudia had gotten a call from the Portland International Airport manager saying the vice president had landed. Since it was not scheduled, the manager figured the mayor would want to know.

He was right, of course. But Alan Wallace's presence in

the city made getting work done even harder. Claudia and Janet spent another half hour trying to figure out just why he was in town. Again, no luck.

Then, slightly before three an aide for the vice president called and said he was heading for the mayor's office and asked if it would be possible for a meeting. Claudia said yes without even asking Janet. She knew what Janet would say without a doubt.

Ten minutes later the handsome Alan Wallace, vice president of the entire country, walked into Janet's office and introduced himself. Claudia had never met the man before, and her first thought was that he was even more striking in person than on television.

With him was a stern-looking man by the name of Robert Earhart, the regional director of the FBI.

After the introductions were finished and both men were seated, Claudia stood behind and to the right of Janet's desk.

"Thanks for seeing us on short notice," Alan Wallace started off. Then the smile dropped from his face. "We have a very, very serious situation that has developed in your beautiful city."

Janet had been leaning back in her chair slightly, doing her best to look calm. But with the vice president's words she sat straight up. "What situation?"

"I understand," Earhart said, "that your stepuncle, one Albert Hancer, is missing from a nursing home."

Claudia could feel the shock make her face go slack, and she quickly recovered. The vice president of the United States was asking about Janet's stepuncle. What for?

Janet only nodded, obviously as stunned by the question as Claudia felt.

"Well," he said, "either your stepuncle, or more likely a

copy of your stepuncle, was found in a hotel room this afternoon with an armed hydrogen bomb."

Janet came out of her chair like a shot. "What?"

Claudia's mind took a fraction of a second longer to actually hear what the vice president had said. Then she was standing beside Janet, both of them towering over the two seated men.

Earhart held up his hands and Claudia stepped back. Janet managed to sit down again. "Everything is being done that can be done at the moment," Earhart said. "The FBI is working on getting the bomb out of the city. We will inform you as soon as that has occurred. But in the meantime, for obvious reasons, this news cannot go any farther than this office."

Janet nodded. "Do you know who's behind this? It couldn't have been Albert."

"We have some theories," Alan Wallace said. "But we know your stepuncle had nothing to do with it. He will be taken out of the city for tests. You will be kept informed of his progress."

Janet nodded. Claudia could tell she was shocked. And with good reason. "Sir, how was the bomb found?"

Earhart looked at Claudia, then back at Janet and smiled. "The investigator you hired to find Albert found it. Lucky for all of us that he did."

"McCallum," Claudia said. It would figure he'd be in the middle of all this. He always seemed to be.

The vice president stood, and with him both Janet and Earhart. "I wish there was more we could say at the moment," he said. "My office will keep you completely informed as to the developments."

Janet nodded and Claudia found herself nodding also, almost like a zombie.

"I assume," Earhart said, "that we have your silence on this problem until we tell you otherwise. And your help if needed."

Janet stuck out her hand to the vice president, then Earhart. "Of course."

"Good," Wallace said. "Thanks for your time."

With that he and Earhart turned and left, closing the door behind them.

Claudia went around and slumped down into the chair facing Janet's desk. The same one the vice president had just sat in. For the first time she realized she was actually sweating.

And then the realization that a live hydrogen bomb might go off at any moment hit her. And she began sweating even more.

22

Eliminate the impossible. Then if nothing remains, some part of the "impossible" must be possible.

—ANTHONY BOUCHER
FROM *ROCKET TO THE MORGUE*

2:50 P.M. JUNE 24.
PORTLAND, OREGON

It had now been twenty minutes since Earhart had left to talk to the vice president. McCallum had spent most of the time watching as the two men studied the hydrogen bomb in the suitcase. So far they hadn't actually touched the suitcase, and Albert Hancer had yet to take his gaze from it. The more McCallum studied the situation, the more uneasy he got with the entire thing. Earhart had ruled out medical help for Albert until they took care of the bomb, and McCallum had agreed that was a sound idea. It almost seemed as if the old guy was guarding the bomb.

Over the last hour in the room McCallum had somehow gotten used to the smell, or at least his nose had gone dead on him. And the heat had been reduced when Henry went out and propped the front door of the hotel open downstairs, and opened a window leading into the alley at the end of the hall upstairs. A good breeze now swirled through, taking the heat, and maybe some of the smell, with it.

Henry had come back laughing. "There's about a hundred men in suits scattered up and down the street outside," he said. "Not too obvious or what?"

Henry went to the foot of the bed and began talking with Dr. Cornell. The two technicians brought in by FBI Regional Director Earhart continued to study the bomb. And Neda Foster paced in and out of the room, making arrangements to have Albert Hancer transported north.

McCallum thought the time went by in a strangely normal way, considering that they all might die at any moment. And they wouldn't even know what hit them.

Finally McCallum couldn't contain his uneasiness about the bomb situation. He stopped Neda Foster on one of her trips into the room. "I would suggest that you have Albert, there, in securely tied bonds before you touch that suitcase."

Neda looked from Albert to the suitcase and back again. "I've been worried about that," she said. "Good idea. I'll get the rope."

McCallum's stomach still didn't settle. "You also might try moving them together, never letting Albert's gaze off the suitcase."

"We need to get this bomb out of the city fast," Neda said. "We're airlifting it off the roof here in about five minutes, as soon as Earhart gets back, flying it straight out over the ocean to a Navy research ship."

"I'd be real careful," McCallum said. "If that really is some sort of *thing*, as your Dr. Cornell seems to think, it most likely is programmed to defend the suitcase. And since you haven't told me who did this, I have no idea what sort of defense it might have available to it."

"Trust me," Neda said. "You wouldn't believe me if I told you."

"I can believe a lot of things," McCallum said.

Neda Foster laughed, a short choppy laugh that ended almost in a disgusted snort. "Yeah," she said. "Tell you what I will do. If we make it out of this alive, you come up to my facility in Bellingham tomorrow and I'll do my best to convince you."

McCallum was about to agree to her invitation when Earhart entered the room. Behind him was a tall man dressed in a suit. The guy looked familiar to McCallum, but it took a few moments before it dawned on him that it was the vice president of the entire damn country. And he was walking right into a room with a bomb.

Henry's face went white, and McCallum knew he had almost as shocked a look on his face. What the hell was the vice president doing walking into a room with a live hydrogen bomb? What exactly was going on here?

The vice president put his hand over his nose and closed his eyes at the first sight of Albert Hancer. "That's the clone?" he asked.

"Not really a clone, sir," Dr. Cornell said. "More of a growth of a mass of organic tissue that looks and pretends to be human."

"Has it moved?" the vice president asked.

"Except for the breathing motion, that is only cosmetic," Dr. Cornell said, "it has not."

"And that's the bomb?" he asked, pointing to the suitcase standing between two equipment cases.

"That's it, sir," Earhart said. "We're going to airlift it out over the ocean as soon as you are clear of the city."

"You're not going to wait one more minute," the vice president said. "I'll not have you risking one more life just because I'm stupid enough to come in here. Understand?"

"Yes, sir," Earhart said. He moved to the door and spoke to a man standing out in the hallway. "Signal for the chopper to come in."

"You need to restrain Albert there," McCallum said, making his tone very insistent. "Don't let them touch that bomb without having him under total control."

"Agreed," Neda said.

Earhart nodded and turned to the man out in the hall again. "Rope, handcuffs, and a large blanket. Quickly."

The vice president turned to McCallum. "I assume you're the man who found this?"

McCallum nodded and stuck out his hand. "Richard McCallum, sir. I'm having a hard time believing that you're in here with this thing."

The vice president laughed. "Actually, so am I. But I was in the neighborhood."

McCallum laughed. "Not a very good neighborhood, sir."

"I'll agree with that," the vice president said. "Has Neda brought you up to speed on what all this is about?"

"I'm afraid not," McCallum said. "She's promised me a briefing if I go up to Bellingham tomorrow."

"Go," the vice president said. "We're going to need all the good people we can get on this."

A man in a suit appeared with a rope, handcuffs, and a blanket and handed them to Earhart.

"Let me have the rope," Henry said, and the regional

director of the FBI handed it to him as if he were a traffic cop being ordered around.

Henry quickly tied one end of the rope into a large slip-knot, then, nodding to McCallum, dropped it quickly over Albert's head.

There was no reaction.

Henry quickly pulled the rope tight, then with quick motions wound the rope around and around Albert, trapping his arms against his sides.

"I'll see if I can get those handcuffs on his wrists now," Henry said.

"Use gloves," Dr. Cornell almost screamed, jumping in close to the bed. "The skin material may be acid."

"Thanks for warning me before now, Doc," Henry said, giving Cornell one of his nastiest looks.

The doctor half grinned at Henry as he handed him a pair of thin gloves from his pocket. "I just thought of it."

Henry put the gloves on, then slowly eased Albert's wrists behind his back until the handcuffs were in place.

"God, his skin feels like a slug," Henry said, standing back and holding his gloved hands away from his body after he was finished. "Slimy. And almost loose. I'm going to have nightmares about this for weeks."

"We all are," the vice president said.

McCallum could see that where Henry had touched Albert's skin there were clear marks where the skin had just slipped off, or was pushed back. Red drops of blood were welling up, but he wasn't really bleeding like a cut would bleed.

The doctor held out a plastic bag for the gloves. "Drop them in here."

Somehow Henry managed to get the gloves off without

touching the outsides of them, and the doctor had the bag sealed and labeled in a flash.

"Help me with this," Henry said, glancing at McCallum.

McCallum moved up and grabbed an end of the blanket.

"On the count of three," Henry said, "we put it over him and wrap it to the right."

"When we put the blanket over him," McCallum said, "is when we're going to have the problem, if we're going to have one. The blanket will block his view of the suitcase. If he's guarding the thing he's going to fight."

Henry nodded and with that said, "One. Two. Three!"

They pulled the blanket over Albert's head and then down hard. Then, as if in one motion, they wrapped the blanket to the right, making a cocoon around Albert, twisting him back so he was laid out on the bed.

For a moment there was a thrashing under the blanket, but nothing like McCallum had handled dozens of times with drugged-up crooks. He and Henry had no problem holding Albert.

Then the form they were holding suddenly went limp.

There was a loud hissing sound from under the blanket. Both Henry and McCallum jumped back, letting go, as if a snake was about to come out of there.

Then, where there had been the shape of a man, there was suddenly nothing.

The blanket sort of sunk in on itself.

"I was afraid that might happen," Dr. Cornell said.

"What might happen?" Henry screamed at the doctor.

"This," Cornell said. He moved up and pulled back a corner of the blanket. Arthur's clothes were still there, soaked in a pool of slimy white liquid.

"My God," the vice president said. "I don't think I really believed all this was true until this very moment."

"Get that bomb out of here!" Earhart said. "And fast!"

That was the first time McCallum had heard Earhart sound more than bored. Now there was a panicked look in the cold eyes of the regional director.

The two technicians simply picked up the suitcase between them and, following Earhart, headed down the hall at a fast walk toward the stairs to the roof.

Now only Henry, Cornell, the vice president, and Neda Foster remained in the hot, stinking room with McCallum. He couldn't believe what he had just seen happen. He would have bet any amount of money that had been a real person sitting on the bed. A very sick person, but a real one. But Cornell had been right. It had been something else.

None of this was possible.

Henry glanced down at the pool of white slime on the bed and then back up at Neda Foster. "Someone want to tell me what exactly just happened?"

"Come up to my lab in Bellingham tomorrow and I'll do my best to explain it all," Neda Foster said.

"And Detective, that was a fine job," the vice president said.

"Thank you, sir," Henry said. "But I've never had one melt on me before."

The vice president half laughed, then grew serious. "Remember to keep this quiet. This never happened. Understand?"

Henry nodded.

The vice president turned to McCallum. "And you?"

McCallum forced a strained laugh out of his throat. "Who would believe me if I told them?"

23

Fear is a tyrant and despot, more terrible than the rack, more potent than the snake.

—EDGAR WALLACE
FROM *THE CLUE OF THE TWISTED CANDLE*

7:00 P.M. JUNE 24.
LOCATION UNKNOWN

Tina Harris's counting was interrupted as the newcomer to the caves staggered past her and sat down hard against the cave wall, three paces away.

The heat was finally starting to subside and she had somehow managed to make it through another day. The light coming in from the crack above was starting to dull. It was evening now outside. She still wasn't sure why she was fighting so hard to stay alive when so many others around her had died.

But she was.

She moved to stretch her cramped legs and arms, a moan escaping from her dried throat as she did so. She was so caked with dirt that it cracked and flaked off as she moved.

The newcomer had been dumped in earlier in the day and had woken up a few hours back, loudly demanding to know what was going on. An older man near the door had explained it the best he could, just loud enough so that most of the rest of them in the cave could hear. As far as Tina was concerned, he hadn't missed a thing.

Tina stared at the new man. He was naked, as they all were, but somewhat cleaner. He seemed about her age, from what she could tell. He sat against the wall, one hand covering his crotch with the other pressed over his eyes. She had a faint memory, from five or so days ago, that she too had been concerned about being naked in front of others. She hadn't thought about it now in days. It seemed like such a small detail when compared to finding a way to stay alive.

"You all right?" she said, her voice oddly harsh and raspy in her throat.

The guy nodded and pulled his hand away from his eyes. "This is a nightmare. I fell climbing down into the canyon, hit my head, and am having a nightmare. That has to be it. And any moment now I'm going to wake up in a hospital."

"If so," Tina said, "I wish you'd hurry and wake up. I don't know how many more days of this I can take."

For the first time the guy actually seemed to look at her. Then he nodded. "I'll do my best."

After a moment of quiet he said, "My name's Cobb. I live on a ranch near here."

"Tina," she said. Then it dawned on her what he had said. "How do you know where we are?"

Cobb laughed, a half bitter, half crying laugh. "I was coming to these caves to explore with a friend. I don't know what those creatures—aliens—whatever they are, did with him. I grew up exploring these caves."

"You're kidding," Tina said. "Where are we?"

Cobb indicated the cave around them. "This is a small side tunnel off the main Sheepeater Cave. We're in eastern Oregon near Hells Canyon."

"High desert," Tina said to herself. "That explains why it's so damn hot."

"It's a bunch hotter outside than in here," Cobb said.

"So, is there a back way out of here?" Tina asked. She knew the answer, but for some reason it felt good to ask. As if asking was convincing herself that she was working to escape.

Cobb laughed. "If there is, it's right about where we're both sitting."

She looked at him hard, her mind clearing by the moment. "How do you know that?"

He pointed at the roof of the cave. "See how this is longer than it is wider, running from the front to here?"

She glanced back at the area that the aliens had blocked off. He was right. It was almost more of a tunnel than a cave. She had paid no attention before.

"These caves were formed when molten lava in tubes running underground cooled, leaving air bubbles. Sometimes these lava tubes can go for miles. Other times they end like this."

"So there is no back way out," she asked.

He looked around where he was sitting. "If there is, it's buried under this dirt." He patted the ground. "I suppose, given a little time, we might be able to move a little to see. My brothers and I dug out the ends of a few caves and found more tunnels beyond. But if we did find something, there would be no telling where it would lead."

She looked at him for a moment, then shifted forward and pulled out one of her bottles of water from where she'd hidden it near the rock. She flipped it to him. "Take a very small drink. They've given us water and food every day, but you never know."

For a moment Cobb looked as if he might cry, then nodded to her. "Thanks." He took a very small drink and handed it back.

She placed the bottle under her and then slowly, while there was still some light, began studying the end of the cave, looking for the most likely place to dig.

Three paces from her, Cobb did the same thing.

24

The worst is so often true.

—DAME AGATHA CHRISTIE
FROM *THEY DO IT WITH MIRRORS*

7:30 P.M. JUNE 24.
PORTLAND, OREGON

Neda Foster sat on a leather couch in Air Force Two at the Portland International Airport. Across from her the vice president sat in a large, overstuffed leather chair. It was clearly a chair designed for him and he looked comfortable in it. Finishing out the group was Regional Director of the FBI Earhart, sitting in a chair facing Alan Wallace, talking softly on a phone.

When they'd first boarded the plane she had washed up and Alan had the air-conditioning turned up. Alan also had his staff bring in a light dinner and coffee. The three of them had managed to go the few minutes it took to eat without talking about the day's events.

Earhart clicked his phone off and smiled at Alan. "They disarmed the bomb."

Neda felt a huge wave of relief sweep over her. They had gotten lucky this time. Very, very lucky. Now they needed to keep moving and see if they could stop the Klar. Then she remembered why they had gone to Portland and the relief quickly left her.

"Great!" the vice president said. "Did they find out anything about it?"

Earhart nodded. "Totally alien construction, yet made with materials from right here on Earth. It packed pretty much the power of one of ours, but was designed to emit an extra-high level of EMP."

The vice president nodded. "To destroy the center of the city and make all electronic equipment useless for hundreds of miles around. That would have ground everything to a halt here in Oregon quite fast."

"Exactly," Earhart said. "It was lucky we found the thing when we did."

The relief that Neda had felt a moment before was now flipped into total despair. When she had talked to the vice president this morning and called in his help, she had only told him that they had a lead on a possible alien plot to destroy Portland. She hadn't told him everything.

The plane around her seemed to spin as she fought to catch a breath. The aliens were going to destroy the entire world and it was going to happen at any moment. And there didn't seem to be anything she could do about it, even though she now knew how they were planning to do it.

Her face must have shown her dismay. Alan sat up straight and leaned toward her. "Neda? Are you all right?"

She shook her head no. Somehow she had to stop her

head from spinning and tell him the entire truth. Somehow.

"It's over for the moment, Neda," Alan said. "We got a jump on them."

"No," she managed to say, her voice shaky-sounding to her ears. She took a deep breath and the inside of the plane seemed to slow some. Another deep breath and she had her control back. "No, Mr. Vice President, we didn't."

"I'm not following you," he said.

"We disarmed the bomb," Earhart said. "What more could there be?"

Neda glanced at the regional director, then faced the vice president. "I didn't tell you this morning, but the reason we knew to look in Portland for an elderly man was because there have been elderly people abducted by the Klar near *every* major city in the world over the last six days. Portland was just close and small enough to search quickly."

"Every city?" Earhart said. "How do you know that?"

Neda watched the vice president's face turn pasty white as the information she had told him soaked in. "Mr. Earhart," she said. "My organization is very well funded and has spent the last six years doing nothing but tracking Klar abductions and researching the Klar. We have operatives in every major police force in the world, including the FBI and CIA. Plus we know exactly what to look for."

She took a deep breath and went on, ignoring the shocked look on Earhart's face. "Lately the Klar have become almost careless, not really caring who sees them abduct an elderly person. Albert Hancer was lifted from the center court of a walled nursing home with four witnesses."

"They're acting as if it soon won't matter very much?" the vice president asked.

"It would seem that way," Neda said. "And that is not like them at all."

"Every major city?" Earhart said, more to himself than anyone else.

"Yes, sir," Neda said. "Almost ever major city."

Earhart shook his head from side to side. "I've got myself very confused. Would you go over *exactly* why these Klar are doing this? And *why*, in God's name, they're using elderly?"

Neda glanced at Alan, then nodded. "The Klar having been watching us, abducting us, and studying us for about fifty years, looking for a way to control us, beat us into submission, take over this planet. But they have a very large problem. They only arrived with about twenty ships."

"Twenty?" Earhart asked.

"Twenty," Neda said. "And they are a very careful race. In fifty years they have never allowed anything of theirs to get into human hands. Ever."

"Okay," Earhart said, "so they want the planet, but that doesn't explain why the elderly."

Neda smiled. "The Klar stay very hidden, and never get near the lights and people of large cities. So obviously when they came up with the idea of bombing our cities, they needed something, or someone to haul their bombs."

"Something, or someone, that wouldn't be obvious," Alan said.

"Homeless elderly," Earhart said, nodding in understanding.

"Exactly," Neda said. "Before this they always abducted younger people to study, or to be used as slaves as I was for a time. So when they started taking the elderly near each city, we knew something was different."

"Very good thinking on your part," Earhart said.

Neda felt her stomach clamp up again. "But not fast enough, it seems."

"So what are they waiting for?" the vice president asked.

"We know, sir," Neda said, "that the abductions of the elderly are still taking place. Most likely they're just not ready yet."

"So we tipped our hand today?" Earhart said.

Neda shook her head. "I don't think so. The Klar are very, very careful and there just aren't that many of them. Until I saw the thing-on-the-bed today, we didn't think the Klar had any way of infiltrating our society. They've been around Earth for over fifty years and chances are they won't move until they are absolutely sure of destroying everything that might have a chance of stopping them. Building those *things* might take them some time."

"Either way," Alan said, "It's only a matter of a few days, a week at most."

Neda nodded. "I'm afraid so. The *thing* that looked like Albert Hancer paid two weeks rent on that room."

"That only leaves eight to ten days on the outside," the vice president said.

"Every major city in the world," Earhart said again, as if trying to make the enormity of that fact sink in.

"Every major city," Neda replied.

25

It's dangerous, very dangerous . . . to go from a preconceived idea to find the proofs to fit it.

—GASTON LEROUX
FROM *THE MYSTERY OF THE YELLOW ROOM*

8:10 A.M. JUNE 25.
BELLINGHAM, WASHINGTON

McCallum thought the waiting room at Neda Foster's offices was small for someone with her and her father's money.

Five fake-wood chairs, a few magazines, and a metal desk, clearly not used often, were crammed into the space. Worn, brown indoor-outdoor carpeting covered the floor and there were a few plastic plants that filled the corners, mostly covered with dust. No background music filled the room like a normal waiting room, and occasionally a loud thump could be heard from behind the metal door. There was no doubt that Neda Foster very seldom entertained visitors at this location.

A man with long hair and thick glasses in a white lab

coat had said Neda Foster would be right with them, and then had left through the heavy metal door behind the desk. Henry dropped into one of the chairs and picked up an old copy of *National Geographic*. McCallum knew Henry was as bothered and nervous as he felt. But Henry very seldom showed it.

McCallum sometimes did. And this was one of those occasions. He chose to pace and think, walking back and forth in front of Henry.

He, Henry, Claudia, and the mayor had had dinner together the previous evening. McCallum and Henry had filled the two women in on what had happened in the small room; and Janet had relayed what had been said in her meeting with the vice president, and also when he called her to say that the bomb had been defused. They had all toasted with champagne when that call came in.

But the celebration had felt hollow to McCallum. And sleep hadn't come at all. Claudia had stayed with him and she'd woken up screaming from nightmares twice.

The entire evening of talking about the day's events had left him even more confused and worried. Albert Hancer was abducted out of a closed courtyard.

How? And by whom?

Then some sort of copy of him turns up with an armed hydrogen bomb in downtown Portland. How was that thing-on-the-bed built? And why bomb Portland? McCallum could think of about a hundred cities more likely to be bombed than Portland, Oregon.

The only thing McCallum could figure was that there was some sort of major terrorist threat happening behind the scenes in this country. And somehow he had managed to stumble into it yesterday.

After he and Claudia had gotten back to his apartment

he had called Tina Harris's father and asked for another early morning use of the Harris corporate jet. He told Harris that there might be a lead in Bellingham and that he and Henry needed to fly up there for an early morning meeting. Harris said the jet would be standing by at seven and would wait for them to return.

McCallum continued his pacing in the waiting room in front of Henry, thinking about everything.

He actually hadn't lied to Harris. There were unsettling similarities between his two missing persons cases that he couldn't get out of his head. He hoped that Neda Foster might put some sort of light onto what had happened the day before. And he hoped that light might give him a lead to Tina Harris and the real Albert Hancer. But his twisting stomach told him that wasn't going to happen.

Behind the desk the door opened and Neda Foster came through. She looked tired and her blond hair had clearly been pulled back quickly, without thought. Her appearance didn't settle McCallum's worries in the slightest.

"Thanks for coming," she said, reaching out and shaking both their hands. "Sorry to keep you waiting, but we're in a sort of panic around here. I haven't slept since yesterday."

"Trust me," Henry said. "The nightmares weren't worth going to sleep for."

"More developments?" McCallum asked.

Neda nodded. "It seems events are moving faster than any of us had ever imagined." She pointed to waiting-room chairs. "Have a seat. Before we go inside the lab there are a few things I must first try to tell you."

Henry dropped down into the chair he'd just left and McCallum sat one away from him. Neda took a chair and swung it around so that she could sit facing them.

McCallum could tell she was clearly forcing herself to

stop and spend a few minutes with them. But the energy of needing to keep working showed up in her constant movement.

She took a deep breath and started talking fairly fast. "Normally I would spend more time setting up a person for the shock of what I'm about to say. But after yesterday, I don't have the time."

"I'd say after yesterday we're pretty open to explanations," McCallum said.

"Boy, are we," Henry said.

Neda smiled a strained smile. "I'm hoping that's the case. So I'm going to make a long story very short. Years ago I was hiking along a trail near Mount Rainier with my boyfriend. It was nearing dark and we were in a hurry to get back to the car, since we hadn't brought camping equipment. We were within a hundred yards of our car when a white light covered us both."

"White light?" Henry asked, giving Neda a chance to take a breath. "From where?"

"From above," Neda said. "Just as the witnesses said in the Albert Hancer disappearance."

McCallum said nothing as she stared at him, so she went quickly on.

"The white light froze us in our tracks, as though someone had taken control of our bodies. We couldn't move a muscle. My scientists have a theory that the white light contains a high-speed strobe effect that somehow short-circuits the pathways between the brain and the muscles in a human body. But so far we haven't been able to duplicate the effect."

"Hell of a weapon if you ever do," Henry said.

"So what happened next?" McCallum asked.

"I passed out," Neda said. "And when I awoke I was in

an old mine shaft, totally naked, with about ten other men and women. My boyfriend was not with me. Most of the others were near death. The dirt floor in that mine was cold and damp. I still, to this day, have trouble staying warm."

"So who abducted you?" McCallum asked. "And why?"

"The Klar," Neda Foster said. "As for why? I have no idea. Study, most likely, although they did force me to haul boxes one day."

"Who are the Klar?" Henry asked. He glanced at McCallum and then back at Neda.

"I think who the Klar are is the point of all this," McCallum said. He had a very strong suspicion where all this was heading. She was going to tell them she had been abducted by aliens. And McCallum was already having a hard time buying this. But after what happened yesterday in that room in the Sundown Hotel, he was listening. That was more than he ever would have done before yesterday.

"That I'll show you in just a moment," she said, nodding to McCallum. "But let me continue with my story. I was in that cave for three days. Days that seemed to be an eternity."

McCallum could see her eyes glaze slightly, and her voice shook a little as the memory of those days returned. She had obviously dealt with the event, but it was still clearly painful for her to speak about.

"During those three days I was taken out of the mine three times by the Klar. I was always knocked unconscious first, but I woke up each time on a hospital-like table, under white light, with the Klar standing over me."

She took a deep breath to focus herself, then went on. "On the fourth morning, one of the others in the mine discovered some loose boards near the back of the old tunnel. The boards led to another side shaft. Four of us had enough energy left to crawl through and try to escape. Obviously the Klar had not really explored their prison very well."

"So four of you escaped?" Henry said.

"Only two of us eventually made it," Neda said. "We stumbled around in miles of old tunnels in pitch blackness. It seemed like an eternity, but it must have been close to two days. We were in constant fear of the Klar catching us. During those hours in the blackness we lost two somewhere in the branching tunnels, but a woman by the name of Cindy and I managed to stay together. We somehow found the way out a side tunnel."

"Was this an old gold mine?" McCallum asked.

"Silver," she said. "The Brandon Mine to be exact, on the south slope of Mount Rainier. The police went back there, but there was nothing to be found."

McCallum nodded. Old silver mines sometimes had miles of dirt tunnels and dozens of openings. "Go on," he said.

"It was night when we found the secondary opening. We were surrounded by trees and brush. We stayed in the tunnel until well after daylight, since we knew the Klar move around at night. Then we made a run for it down the mountain. Three hours later we found a highway. It was a shock to the poor motorist who stopped for two dirty, naked, and bleeding women, I'll tell you."

McCallum said nothing. At this point he was just waiting. Neda was going to show them something very shortly inside that lab, and this story was trying to prepare them for it. So he would listen, without comment until the right time.

"I never saw my boyfriend again," she said. "Using my father's money, the next year I began this organization to track abductions nationally, and now worldwide. We also have done thousands of studies on the Klar, what we know of their technology, and their possible plans. The Klar are the ones who built that Hancer look-alike and planted that bomb yesterday."

"And the government is in on all this," Henry said.

"Now," Neda Foster said. "But up until a few days ago they were not. We have always been an entirely privately funded organization. And as of this moment, the president still does not know. The vice president and a select group of others are planning to tell him of the Portland event and other developments this afternoon."

"The president doesn't know we almost lost an American city?" McCallum asked. He was actually shocked at that news. He would have assumed the president was being informed the entire time.

"Amazing," Henry said.

"There's more to it than just one city," Neda said.

"Oh," Henry said, looking at her with a puzzled expression on his face.

"Okay," McCallum said, ignoring the fear he felt in response to her comment. "After yesterday and that personal background, I think we're ready to see what's behind that door."

Neda Foster laughed and quickly stood. "I hope so. We can use all the help we can get at the moment."

She turned and led the way, not waiting for them to follow. She pushed open the heavy metal door behind the desk and stepped through and to the side. They were in an airlock-like room, painted pure white. No windows at all, but state-of-the-art security cameras in two corners.

Neda closed the outer door behind them and punched a code into a panel near the inner door. After a moment the door clicked and opened quietly.

She walked inside a few steps and then moved sideways.

McCallum was a few paces behind her and made it three steps into the giant room before stopping cold.

Behind him, Henry said, "Oh, shit!"

The room was a warehouse-sized space, with high ceilings and what seemed like hundreds of desks and lab tables. Computers and other high-tech equipment seemed to fill every space and people in white coats worked at a frantic pace throughout. But what stopped McCallum were the two statues that stood on a high platform against one wall. The statues were elevated so that they could be seen from every place in the room.

Statues of two monsters.

There was no other way for McCallum to describe them. Pure, Hollywood-looking monsters standing up there like they owned the place. It was right out of a science fiction movie.

"Those are actual-size statues of the Klar," Neda said. "Eight feet tall."

"The Klar actually look like that?" Henry said, his voice a hoarse whisper.

"As close as anyone can get to what the Klar really look like," Neda said. "I use the statues shamelessly to recruit help, just as I'm doing now."

McCallum glanced at her and she shrugged. "A person does what a person has to do."

"I got the idea out of a movie." She looked up at the monsters. "Plus, those statues remind all of us in here what we're fighting."

McCallum laughed. "I can see how it would. They're damn tough to miss."

He turned to stare at the huge statues that dominated the room. Both fake aliens had hoof-like feet, but around the head and shoulders they looked almost snake-like, with two intense black eyes and two slits below the eyes that appeared to be nostrils. Their mouths slanted downward in the largest frown McCallum had ever seen. Their heads were cone-shaped and positioned forward of their bodies on thick, wide necks. Their necks were cords of thick muscles, far wider than their heads, which gave them the cobra-like look. They had intricate patterns on their neck and head, and four arms ending in four claw-like fingers, the two smaller arms tucked under the larger ones. Both wore some sort of a tight-fitting uniform.

"Okay," McCallum said, turning back to Neda. "How long have they been on Earth? How many are there? What do they want? You know, all the standard questions I'm sure all your possible recruits ask."

"Yeah," Henry said. "Good questions."

Neda smiled at them and motioned that they should follow her. She indicated two chairs in front of a cluttered desk near a huge map of the world. Lights and about a thousand pins decorated the map. The room was full of a constant noise of talking, computers and printers humming, phones ringing, and people moving around. It was if they were in the middle of a busy train station.

They both sat down, but it felt to McCallum as if the two monsters were standing right over him. It made him uneasy and he didn't like being emotionally manipulated as Neda was doing to him at the moment.

He didn't like it much at all.

"To answer your questions as best I can," Neda said as she sat down, "they have been watching the planet Earth, from what we can tell, for about fifty years. We think they have twenty ships with about fifty crew per ship. Their ships are basically round, pure black, untrackable by radar, and about fifty feet shorter in diameter than a 747. As for what they want?" Neda paused. "It seems pretty clear, after yesterday, that they want to take over the planet."

She stood. "I want to show you this." She moved around her desk to the large map of the world.

McCallum and Henry stood and moved over beside her.

"By our best count," Neda said, "the Klar have averaged about three hundred abductions of humans worldwide per year over the last twenty-five years. Some of the humans are put back into society. A few of us escape. Most just disappear. People of all ages, sizes, and nationalities."

McCallum knew how large the missing persons files were in the Portland police records. He could believe three hundred worldwide per year. It wouldn't even dent the total.

"However," Neda said, "over the last eight days elderly men have been abducted near every major city in the world. Men such as Albert Hancer."

She pointed at the map. "All the red flags are elderly men missing in those eight days."

McCallum studied the map for a moment. There was a red flag sticking out of ever major city on the map.

"All for carrying bombs?" Henry said.

"It seems that way," Neda said. "You know the bomb yesterday was defused. What you don't know is that it was of alien construction and designed to emit an extreme amount of EMP."

"EMP?" Henry asked, glancing at McCallum for an explanation. Since McCallum read so much, Henry always looked to him to explain weird terms. And this one he happened to know.

"Electromagnetic pulse," McCallum said. "It burns out all electronic equipment within its range."

"Correct," Neda said.

"Why?" Henry said, still not clearly catching the reason for doing such a thing.

"All electronic equipment," McCallum said. "Electronic ignition and fuel injection in cars, all computers, all bank records, just about everything we use, including communications systems and doughnut makers."

"Oh," Henry said, a look of understanding crossing his face.

"So," McCallum said, turning back to Neda, "the bombs take out the populations of the major cities and the EMP takes out the rest of the civilization in the area around the cities. And the bombs are being smuggled into the cities by copies of elderly people. Right?"

"On the money," Neda said. "And from the information we got yesterday, it's all going to blow sometime in the next six to twelve days."

"Shit!" Henry said.

McCallum didn't know what to say. If he hadn't seen a body dissolve in his hands, and the vice president and the regional director of the FBI taking this seriously, yesterday, he'd be laughing at the moment.

He didn't believe all that Neda was saying, but he was a long, long way from laughing.

26

The terrier does not give the rat time to dig a hole.

—LESLIE THOMAS
FROM *ORMEROD'S LANDING*

9:06 A.M. JUNE 25.
SHEEPEATER CAVES, EASTERN OREGON

Tina Harris, with Cobb, had spent part of the night digging and trying to move rocks near the back of the cave. Even being careful not to make much of a mess, and working in the total darkness, they had managed to find a small hole going under the back wall of the cave. They didn't have the time to open it up to find out if it was big enough to crawl through. And there was no telling how far back it went. Most likely the hole dead-ended in five feet. But it was more of a chance to get out of there than Tina had had the day before.

As the first light from the sunrise filtered through the crack in the roof they had managed to make the area where they had been working look almost normal, moving a large rock over in front of the hole. Then Cobb had sat on the rock, leaning against the back of the cave while Tina had gone back to the rock she had used the last few days.

From where she sat it was impossible to tell that any digging had been done. Now she hoped that if the aliens came in, they wouldn't be able to tell either. And if they were coming it would be in the early morning hours. At least, over the last six days it had happened that way.

She leaned against the cool rock, letting herself relax a little. Her hands were sore and three of her fingers were bleeding. She had also dropped a rock on the top of her foot and it hurt like hell. All around she felt tired, more tired than she could ever remember feeling. But she really didn't care. This was a good tired. She knew she'd make it through the heat of the day, even though she had less than one bottle of water left. She'd make it through without counting, because today she had some hope.

She smiled at Cobb through the faint morning light and he smiled back.

Then she closed her eyes, letting the exhaustion take her.

27

He who is capable of memory and reason . . . needs no seer's crystal ball.

—LILLIAN DE LA TORRE
FROM *THE CONVEYANCE OF EMELINE GRANGE*

9:10 A.M. JUNE 25.
BELLINGHAM, WASHINGTON

Neda Foster had been called away for a moment by an assistant, leaving McCallum and Henry standing near the huge map of the world. McCallum used the time to look around at the people working at computers and desks. They all had the same harried look Neda Foster had. And a few of them looked as though they were about to explode or break down into tears. McCallum didn't know how he felt. Her explanation seemed rational and logical. And totally far-fetched, even with what he had seen yesterday. He could come up with a half dozen more likely possibilities than aliens.

"What do you think of all this?" Henry said.

McCallum glanced at him. In all the years he had known

Henry he had never heard him say one word about believing in anything beyond his own ability to eat, love his wife and kid, do his job, and maybe start a doughnut shop. Henry wasn't even the type to go to church.

"You know," McCallum said, gazing at where Neda Foster talked impatiently to a man in a white lab coat, "I honestly don't know *what* to think."

"Yeah," Henry said. "But that guy yesterday, melting in that blanket like that. Hard to say I didn't see that. Hell, I was holding him when it happened."

"And that was the vice president," McCallum said. "No doubt about him being there at all. But if that was a real hydrogen bomb, would the vice president be within a thousand miles of it?"

"Yeah," Henry said again. "It was him. But if I were the vice president, I wouldn't have been there, that's for sure."

The low roar of noise in the room around them filled the gap in conversation and McCallum went back to studying the map. It was fairly large, bigger across than most small bedrooms. There were trapdoors in each ocean that opened so that someone could come up from underneath and add pins in the impossible-to-reach locations in the middle. But the size allowed the details of the map to be fairly clear.

The colors of the pins varied, too. Red-topped pins Neda had said were the abductions of the past week. Those red-tops were evenly spaced over the entire map. Then there were green-topped pins, blue pins, and black pins. McCallum had no idea what the colors signified, and there was no one around to ask. He was about to turn and study the two statues of monsters standing against the wall behind him when he noticed two blue pins stuck in central Idaho. He leaned forward, trying to get a better view of exactly where those pins were stuck.

"You interested in something on the map, Mr. McCallum?" Neda Foster asked, turning from her assistant and moving back over near McCallum.

"Those two pins in central Idaho. What do they mean?"

"Blue means that the missing person was highly likely to have been abducted by the Klar," Neda said. She pointed at two pins near the edge. "Green signifies a certain alien abduction, usually meaning there were witnesses. And black means possible abduction, but not enough information."

"Who were the two blue ones in central Idaho?" McCallum asked.

Neda looked at them a moment, then shrugged. "I don't remember. I'll check, if you want."

"Please," McCallum said.

Henry gave McCallum a raised-eyebrow look, following where he was heading with his question.

She moved over to a computer terminal sitting on one edge of the huge map. Her fingers danced over the keys for a moment, then she said, reading off the screen, "Tina Harris and her boyfriend Jerry Rodale. Taken from a camp on the Middle Fork of the Salmon River June 18. No witnesses. They were upgraded from black to blue three days ago when their bodies were not found in the river and no ransom note ever showed up. The file says there is no other likely way they could have gotten out of the valley they were camping in, that their camp was not disturbed, and that there is no background in either family for violence."

Same exact information McCallum had. Amazing.

Then Neda glanced up at McCallum and smiled, then read a line directly off the screen. "Investigator Richard McCallum hired by Harris family to continue search."

McCallum shrugged. "We used the Harris jet to fly up here this morning."

"I can see why you're interested," Neda said. "But unless we can do something about those red pins, you'll never have time to prove us wrong with those two kids, which is what I know you want to do. Right?"

McCallum smiled at her. "More than anything."

"I don't blame you," Neda said. "I'd be doing the same thing in your position."

"So what exactly do you have planned?" Henry asked.

Neda turned and stared at the map. "If the president agrees this afternoon, we're going to start a massive search in every United States city, just as we did in Portland yesterday."

"What about worldwide?" McCallum asked. He couldn't imagine the size undertaking that would be, but it had to be done if what Neda was saying was right.

"I hope so," Neda said. "We already have all our people, and anyone else we can ask, beg, or trick into helping us, searching the cities, starting this morning. If the president gets involved, and we find more bombs, he can talk to other leaders around the world."

"Isn't all this activity going to alert the Klar?" Henry said. "They could just go with the bombs they have planted and work on the other cities later, one at a time."

Neda Foster nodded. "The vice president and I argued about that very point last night. But I believe that the Klar fear us."

"Fear us?" McCallum said, glancing around at the two statues above him. "Why?"

"First, because of the physics of space. We know they are not from our system, which means they came a long way with very few ships to conquer this planet. Most likely it took them hundreds of years to make the trip, and that is if their home world is in the very close galactic neighborhood."

"You're losing me on this space stuff," Henry said.

McCallum had followed her, but not by much. He was glad Henry stopped her at that point.

Neda smiled. "We're sure the Klar have been around Earth for over fifty years, studying us. We also know that their technology is not that far advanced from ours, and we seem to be catching them quickly. Most of our people think the Klar were very surprised when they arrived here and found such an advanced civilization. If a scout ship had been here, say, five hundred years ago, this planet would have looked easy to control. But now, with only twenty of their ships, they wouldn't stand a chance, especially when they arrived to find the war machines of World War Two and the following cold war."

"So they had to find a way to knock us back to the Stone Age," McCallum said.

"And we gave it to them with the electronic age," Neda said. "Take out the population centers and destroy all electronics. Starvation and the nuclear winter would do the rest. Boom! Mankind is back in the Stone Age, ready for easy picking. An entire planet of slaves."

"Yow," Henry said softly.

McCallum shuddered. "All right. I can't say that I totally believe all this, but I'm willing to go along with the threat that I saw yesterday. What can we do?"

Neda nodded. "Thanks. You can do everything you can in Portland."

"But I thought we cleared that yesterday," Henry said.

"If that was a copy of Albert Hancer," McCallum said, "there may be another."

"Exactly," Neda said. "Or they may take another elderly person and make a copy of him. Do whatever you can, short of telling the truth, to get people searching for any possible bombs."

McCallum nodded. "We have the mayor on our side already. We'll guard the city as best we can."

"Thank you," Neda said. "At this point, every city we can protect puts us that much closer to stopping the entire attack."

"Neda," Dr. Cornell yelled from a computer terminal on the other side of the map. "Grab the phone. Quickly!"

She turned and snapped up the phone on her desk. She listened for a moment, then hung up without saying a word. She turned back to McCallum and Henry, a look of total horror on her face.

"They found another bomb," she said, her eyes blank with the shock. "In Tucson. What we feared is the truth. The vice president, the director of the FBI, and my father are meeting with the president."

"Oh, shit," Henry said.

McCallum glanced up at the Klar statues, then back at Neda. This couldn't be happening. There really couldn't be aliens trying to enslave the human race. That was just stuff from the movies. It couldn't happen in real life.

"Good luck, gentlemen," Neda said, moving zombie-like around the desk and dropping down hard into her chair, as if a huge weight was pushing her. "We're all going to need it."

McCallum and Henry both headed for the door at a fast walk. Whether the bombs were being planted by aliens or a terrorist group, Portland was a big city to defend. They were going to need every second they could get to do it.

28

A man's most open actions have a secret side to them.

JOSEPH CONRAD
FROM *UNDER WESTERN EYES*

1:15 P.M. JUNE 25.
WASHINGTON, D.C.

Vice President Alan Wallace sat across the desk from President John Spencer in the Oval Office. Both he and Grant Foster were uncomfortable in the hard-backed chairs, waiting as the president read the FBI report of the happenings in Portland yesterday. But they weren't half as uncomfortable as the head of the FBI, David Barns, who was standing to one side. The president had already chewed him out for not informing him yesterday, when the events were happening.

Alan studied John Spencer as he read. The president was about as opposite to Alan as he could get in body style. While Alan was tall, athletic, and considered good-looking by the press, John stood five four, was more round than thin, and had heavy jowls that gave him a bulldog look. He was also thirty years older than Alan, and almost everyone in the country knew he would never run for a second term.

After the longest five minutes Alan could remember John finally closed the folder and tossed it on the desk in front of him.

"Alan," the president said, his voice controlling anger, "you should be shot for taking a chance like that. If the American people ever found out you walked into a room with an armed hydrogen bomb, they'd impeach you. And most likely me along with you, just for the stupidity of it."

Alan nodded, not willing to say anything. He was much more of a hands-on person than John, and this wasn't the first time John had dressed him down for it. Granted, going into that hotel room had been stupid, but he and John both knew there were much more pressing problems to be dealt with at the moment than his rash judgment calls.

"Now," John said, turning to the director of the FBI. "David, you say your people have found another bomb in Tucson this morning?"

"Yes, sir," FBI Director Barns said. "Same basic facts as the Portland bomb. Same type of bomb. Everything. The bomb is at this moment headed for one of our ships in the Pacific to be disarmed."

"And the elderly person, or thing, with it?"

David Barns looked nervously at Alan for support, then back to the president. "He, or I suppose I should say *it*, melted, sir, after a short struggle. We are testing the remains but, as with the one from Portland, we have no idea what it is, how it could be built, how it operated. In short, we know nothing about him. Or it."

John turned back to face Alan, staring at him with his

intense blue eyes. Those eyes had stared into a million homes through their televisions and gotten the man behind them elected to the world's most powerful office. Now they were directed with full force at Alan. Alan forced himself to return the stare until John spoke.

"Mr. Vice President, you think these snake-looking aliens called Klar are behind these attacks?"

Alan took a deep breath, glanced at Foster, then squarely faced the president. "Sir, I watched that thing melt yesterday in front of my own eyes. I have studied the data supplied by Mr. Foster and his daughter. I have read the reports about the construction of the bomb. Yes sir, I do."

"And you, Mr. Barns?" John asked.

The director of the FBI looked as if he were standing on hot coals as he shifted back and forth. He took a deep breath. "Sir, I honestly don't know what I think at this moment. But the facts are that we have a very large attack going on against this country at this moment, from a force with alien technology. That much I am convinced of. Beyond that . . ." He shrugged helplessly.

The president nodded and pushed himself back in his chair, leaning away from the desk. "I agree with you, Mr. Barns, on the attack. We have a problem and we need to address that, first. And in doing so we will find who's behind it."

John paused for a moment, then went on. "Mr. Vice President, what do you think might be my best course?"

Alan was prepared for this. "Sir, if we truly do have armed hydrogen bombs in every city, as I believe we do at this moment, speed and secrecy are the two factors we need to control."

John nodded agreement as Alan continued.

"We need to mount a massive search in every city for the

bombs, starting at exactly the same moment in every city, most likely tomorrow morning. We need to use mostly local police, with added help from the National Guard and FBI. We need to give them enough powers to break down some doors if needed, but no more information than who they are looking for, and instructions for when they find him."

"Go on," the President said.

"The word *bomb* should never once be mentioned," Alan said. "Never. As well as the world alien. Nothing about either. We let the FBI handle the bombs and man-things when found, without local people involved. And when the press ask what's happening, which they will, we stonewall them until every damn bomb is found."

John nodded. "Mr. Foster, could your organization provide pictures of exactly who we are looking for?"

Foster nodded. "Without problem, sir. We're already double-checking all the cities to make sure we have the right elderly men in each city. Some groups may have to carry two or three pictures of different men, but I don't think that will be a problem."

The president seemed assured. He turned back to the vice president. "Alan, do you think tomorrow morning might be too late?"

Alan shuddered at the question. "Sir, if it is, there's nothing we can do about it now. Some smaller searches are already happening. But it's going to take us that long to set up this size of operation."

"My people," Foster said, "with help from anyone we can find, are mounting searches today throughout the world. But we don't have the manpower to do it right."

"Well, we do," the president said. "Alan, I see no reason to bring the Joint Chiefs in at this point. You and I can brief them later. Much later."

"I look forward to that, sir," Alan said, smiling.

John laughed. "All right," he said, slapping the folder on his desk. "Let's do it."

Alan felt a surge of relief pass through him. Even with two bombs found, there had been no telling what the president would decide to do.

John chuckled to himself. "Everyone knows I've only got one term in me. I might as well go out chasing aliens as anything else. Alan, I want you to write the executive order yourself and have it on my desk here in ten minutes. And I want you to run the operation, keeping me directly informed. You'll need to talk to the mayors and governors. And if any of them give you problems, I'll talk to them. Okay?"

"Yes, sir," Alan said.

"One more thing," John said. "David. Alan. No one outside this room knows of the bombs or mentions the word aliens. I want to keep this job at least through the end of the week. Understood?"

He looked at David and then Alan in turn and each nodded agreement.

"Good hunting, gentlemen," he said. "Now please excuse me. I have a lot of phone calls to make to other world leaders. I need to tell them what's happening, so they can do some searching of their own."

Eight minutes later Alan Wallace handed the president the executive order that would start the biggest search in American history.

The president signed it while talking to the prime minister of Japan.

29

What we were, never was. What we did, never happened.

—DONALD HAMILTON
FROM *DEATH OF A CITIZEN*

2:25 P.M. JUNE 25.
PORTLAND, OREGON

Portland mayor Janet Osborne sat down behind her big desk. Even with her small stature, McCallum was always amazed how *in charge* and powerful she looked there. And what a good job she was doing with the problems of the city.

Claudia stood to Janet's right, leaning against an oak bookshelf full of law books. McCallum, Henry, and Portland Chief of Police Harold Pellegrino sat in chairs facing the mayor.

McCallum had had a busy few hours since his and Henry's return to Portland. He had briefed Tina Harris's father on the chance of a lead, but didn't tell him what it was. Just that there was a lead on his daughter, a slight one, but better than nothing. Mr. Harris had left with a slight glimmer of hope in his eyes. McCallum hoped he hadn't led the man on too much.

Then McCallum had called Earhart at the FBI office in Seattle for any updates, but got nothing from him, as expected. Three more phone calls got the same results, including one to Neda's lab in Bellingham.

Nothing. No news.

Then the mayor had called her meeting.

"I want to remind everyone here," Janet said when everyone was settled, "but mostly you, Chief, that everything said in this room is completely secret, at least for the time being. Maybe forever."

The chief of police nodded as everyone else did. But McCallum could tell he was half insulted by Janet aiming that warning at him. Of course, the chief had very little idea of what was to come next. Actually, neither did Janet and Claudia. But McCallum hadn't decided just how much of the morning visit to Neda Foster's Bellingham lab he was going to tell them about. He'd mentioned that problem to Harry and they'd decided to play it by ear.

"Good," Janet said. "I just got a phone call from the vice president. The president has authorized a countrywide search of every city starting tomorrow morning at eleven eastern time."

"Thank God," Claudia said. The relief in her voice and on her face was exactly how McCallum felt at hearing that news.

"I'll drink to that," Henry said. Actually Henry never drank, but on the plane back this afternoon from Bellingham he had threatened to start. After Neda's story, McCallum was tempted to buy the first bottle and join him.

"Search for what?" the police chief said. "And what does this have to do with finding that guy yesterday?"

"Doesn't know, huh?" McCallum said to Henry, and Henry smiled. It always felt good for a detective to have more information than his chief. It was sort of a job security issue.

"My fault," Janet said, smiling at the chief. "No one but the four of us, the regional director of the FBI, and the vice president knew that an armed hydrogen bomb was found in the Sundown Hotel yesterday."

"What?" the chief shouted at Janet, almost coming out of his chair. He then glanced at Henry. "She's kidding, right?"

"Afraid not, Chief," Henry said. "The FBI flew it to a Navy ship and disarmed it there."

"Why wasn't I informed?" the chief asked.

"National security reasons," the mayor said. "But we'll try to bring you up to speed as quickly as possible."

Her smile pushed the chief of police back into his chair. Janet Osborne had the ability to do that with a smile. McCallum always found it amazing and this time was no exception. She was just a born leader.

"I'm afraid that's not all, Mayor," Henry said, looking at McCallum.

"Henry's right," McCallum said, taking his cue. "Another armed hydrogen bomb was found in Tucson this morning."

This time it was both Janet and Claudia's turn to jump with surprise. Claudia took a step forward, her mouth open to ask a question, then she thought better of it and stepped back.

"So it's happening," Janet said. "Just as Neda Foster feared."

"I'm afraid so," McCallum said.

"Who the hell is doing this?" Janet said, more to herself than anyone in front of her. "I just don't understand."

"Trust me, Mayor," Henry said. "You don't want to know what some people think is behind this."

"Yeah," McCallum said, holding up his hand for Janet to stop before she could ask Henry what he was talking about. "Some people have some wild theories, but for the moment those theories aren't that important. What's important is safeguarding our city. Right?"

Janet studied McCallum's face. She knew he was holding back. He could tell. And he could tell she was trying to decide whether or not to press the issue. Finally she said, "You're right."

"I'm afraid," McCallum said, pushing on, "that we can't assume the city is safe just because we found the one bomb yesterday. There may already be another one planted. Or going to be planted, which I think is more likely."

"Have there been any more elderly men abducted from the area?" Claudia asked.

"I checked the missing person files this afternoon," Henry said. "No elderly man has come up missing besides Albert Hancer in the last month in this area, from Eugene through Vancouver. I checked a one hundred mile radius, including all coastal towns."

"Good," Janet said.

McCallum knew there was something important about what Henry had just said. But for the life of him he couldn't put his finger on it. He made a mental note to come back to it later.

"What does a missing elderly man have to do with the bombs?" the chief asked.

"Someone who looked like Albert Hancer was found with the bomb," Janet said.

McCallum was impressed how she stepped around the thing-on-the-bed problem with that answer.

With the chief still looking puzzled she went on. "The theory is that elderly men are transporting the bombs into the cities using baggage carts. No one notices elderly, or checks them."

"Neda Foster told me this morning," McCallum said, "that they will be sending us pictures tomorrow morning of elderly men gone missing from the Seattle, Tri-Cities, and Boise areas. In the national search tomorrow morning we're to look for them, unless we have a new one of our own."

"Maybe we should stop a new one from happening," Henry said.

"My plan exactly, old partner," McCallum said.

"So maybe you could let the rest of us in on the plan?" Claudia said.

McCallum smiled at her. "Neda's organization learned that almost every elderly person abducted this last week around the world was taken from a nursing home or retirement center. And all were at night."

"So we stake them all out," Henry said. "Every nursing home and retirement center. Simple."

The chief looked at him. "Do you know how many nursing homes and retirement centers there are in this area?"

"Sure do, Chief," Henry said. "It's a three page list. But do you know what a hydrogen bomb would do to this city?"

The police chief's face paled and he said nothing.

McCallum couldn't imagine what the poor chief of police was going to think when he suggested that every stake-out have an antitank weapon with it.

30

When there is only one possibility, it can't be wrong.

—C. DALY KING
FROM *THE CURIOUS MR. TARRANT*

8:03 P.M. JUNE 25.
SHEEPEATER CAVES, EASTERN OREGON

Another day of intense heat had left Tina drained, even though she had slept through most of the day. Her water was almost gone and her stomach ached from hunger. For the first time the aliens hadn't bothered to bring any more food or water and she didn't know why. From what she could tell with a quick look around the cave, another five people had died. Now there were less than twenty with her, and half of those were barely breathing.

A middle-aged woman lying ten feet away was one of the dead. Big black flies buzzed around the curled-up body. Tina wondered for a moment why she was no longer bothered by the smell of the dead. And all the human waste. She couldn't imagine that she had gotten used to the odor.

But it must have happened, because she couldn't smell anything, it seemed.

She stood so she could get a better look around while there was still light. It seemed that she and Cobb were the youngest, and in the best shape by far. It was clearly on their shoulders to go for help if they could. No one else in the cave was going to be able to.

Cobb moved over beside her. He was black with dirt, and a large scrape showed signs of dried blood along his right shoulder. His hair was matted with salt and sweat and his face was almost black.

She imagined she didn't look much better. She didn't even want to look down at her own body to check. It was better at this point that she just keep her body detached from her mind as much as possible. Otherwise the hunger, thirst, and pain would drive her insane.

"I checked out the hole in the light," he whispered. "I can't see the back of it, so it might go into another room. A little bit of widening and I should be able to get through."

"I'm a lot smaller than you are," Tina said. "Could I make it now?"

"I think it's going to take widening for either of us," he said. "But that shouldn't take very long. Maybe an hour or so."

Tina glanced at the light coming in from the crack in the cave roof. "If we start now we might make it with some light to spare."

Cobb nodded. "Exactly what I was thinking."

She bent down and retrieved the last bottle of water from under the rock where she had been sleeping. There was less than a quarter left of it.

She drank half, letting the feel of the water in her throat

fill her every sense for a moment. Then she handed the bottle to Cobb. "Finish it."

"Thanks," he said. She watched as he tipped up the bottle and downed the last of the water, obviously relishing the taste and feel of it as much as she had.

"Okay," he said, tossing the empty bottle down beside a rock. "Let's get to work."

A moment later he was on his stomach, head down into the hole in the rocks, working out stones with his bare hands and passing them back to Tina.

31

Judge not—at least until the evidence is unequivocal.

—COLIN DEXTER
FROM *SERVICE OF ALL THE DEAD*

10:18 P.M. JUNE 25.
PORTLAND, OREGON

McCallum and Claudia sat on folding chairs just inside the glass front door of Hilltop Retirement Center, in the western hills above Portland. From where they sat they could see the front, tree-lined parking lot, and the short front sidewalk. The streetlights cast circles of safety, pushing the darkness back into the surrounding forest.

At McCallum's feet an antitank missile launcher lay waiting, two missiles beside it. McCallum had fired one of the launchers a few years back at an army test show, and had been given a quick refresher course on it when he picked it up at the National Guard armory. "Simply load, aim, and pull the trigger," the soldier had said.

McCallum remembered it not being so easy.

There was one such antitank weapon, with someone who sort of knew how to use it, at each of twenty-six major nursing and rest homes in the Portland area. No one knew what they might be shooting at, but they had permission to use the weapon if someone tried to abduct an elderly man. McCallum shuddered at the thought of an antitank missile accidentally hitting a house, but at the moment none of them, including the mayor, could think of any other choice.

The rest of the nursing homes were guarded by men and women with rifles. McCallum had no idea if rifles would even dent a Klar ship, if such a thing existed. He doubted it. Neda wasn't sure if even an antitank missile would dent one. When he asked, she said, "No one has ever fired at a Klar ship before."

The waiting area around McCallum and Claudia smelled of lilacs and dust. From the neat look of the magazines, no one had used this small waiting area in years. Claudia's right shoe had tapped lightly on the floor for most of the last hour, a nervous habit that McCallum had never noticed in all their years together. He supposed that if any nervous habit was going to come out, it would do so tonight. He wondered what she was noticing for the first time about him.

As they sat there quietly, the words of Dashiell Hammett's character Sam Spade echoed in his head, over and over: *Once a chump, always a chump*. At the moment, he felt like a chump. The chance of anything happening here was beyond slight. He and Henry had spent most of the evening going over the location of each rest home, trying to figure out which would be the most likely for the Klar to hit. They had eliminated all of the homes in the bright, downtown section of the city since Neda said Klar ships never went into cities. Albert Hancer had been taken from a home up in the hills, away from the lights. So they focused there.

The Hilltop Retirement Center was perched near the very top of one of the highest peaks near Portland, tucked back in the pine trees. It was the most logical place for them to watch, and the one McCallum decided he would stake out himself. Henry took the second most logical, just a short distance along the ridge from where McCallum now sat.

McCallum glanced down the hall to his right. He could see one of the national guardsmen standing watch at the side door, his rifle cradled across his arms. There were other guardsmen at the remaining two outside doors, each with rifles. The home's interior garden court had been locked so no one could go out there. None of the guards knew what they were guarding against. They just knew they had to stop anyone or anything that tried to take a resident.

Claudia grabbed McCallum's leg and he turned back to face the front. An old Nash Rambler rolled up the driveway and into the parking lot. Moving slowly it carefully parked in the closest open space to the front sidewalk.

Claudia picked up a paper from the coffee table in front of her and quickly scanned down it, looking for the make of the car to match a resident name. The Hilltop wasn't a nursing home, but more of a managed care facility. Many of the residents had their own cars and were free to come and go as much as they liked.

"That's Mr. Ashley," Claudia said, "coming back from dinner with his family. He's the next to the last one still out."

McCallum bent and picked up the heavy antitank

weapon and one missile. Outside, the sky was pitch black and there was only a sliver of moon to help light the night. If anything was going to happen, it was going to be now.

"Call for the other guards to come down here." They had already done this exact same drill three times in the last hour. Claudia ran into the hall past him as the Nash Rambler's lights clicked off and then the door opened.

Mr. Ashley looked to be in his early seventies. He wore a light brown jacket, dark slacks, and a baseball cap. He remained slightly stooped as he turned and locked up his car. McCallum felt as though he was using Mr. Ashley as bait, but in reality he was only guarding him. If they all walked out there and the Klar were above, the aliens would freeze all of them and that would do no good for anyone.

McCallum laughed at himself. He was thinking as if the Klar really existed. His core belief system knew that wasn't possible. But he was taking no chances. And if that white light was just some terrorist's helicopter picking up people like Albert Hancer, it wasn't going to be in the air long if it came around here.

Beside McCallum, the three guards and Claudia appeared and took up their positions. Claudia picked up the extra missile for the antitank launcher.

McCallum held his breath as the elderly man moved slowly up the sidewalk. The antitank weapon seemed extra heavy in his sweating hands.

Time seemed to stretch.

Mr. Ashley was the slowest human alive. Every step seemed to take a lifetime.

Then the night lit up as if someone had turned the lights on at the baseball park.

And the world went into quick time.

The white light covered the front lawn and sidewalk like an intense spotlight. From where McCallum stood inside, he couldn't see any more than the light coming from the sky.

There was absolutely no noise.

Mr. Ashley froze in mid-stride.

"Go!" McCallum shouted, shoving the first missile in the antitank launcher and pushing his way through the front glass doors as fast as he could go.

He took three steps down the sidewalk, went to one knee, and aimed the antitank weapon at the light overhead. Something huge and black blocked the stars out just above the trees, but McCallum could see nothing of what it was. Just blackness.

There was no noise coming from it.

Nothing but total silence.

This wasn't a helicopter. Or any American plane McCallum had ever heard of.

Mr. Ashley started to lift off the sidewalk as though he weighed nothing and a breeze was pulling him away.

It was now or never. In a moment Mr. Ashley would be too close to the dark shape.

"Fire!" McCallum shouted, and pulled the trigger, aiming directly at the point where the white light came from the dark mass in the sky.

The force of the missile leaving the launcher rocked him back and the heat cut at his face. But he stood his ground.

The missile seemed to have only just left his shoulder when it hit the blackness overhead and exploded.

The flash lit up the underside of the dark mass, showing McCallum strange shapes and diamond patterns on what seemed to be the entire sky above him.

Then the blast concussion knocked him backward into the grass and he ended up tangled with the legs of one of the national guardsmen.

The night went pitch black around them. The blast had knocked out all the streetlights and the home's lights.

The last remains of the blast echoed off over the city below, and then all was silent.

Black and silent.

Mr. Ashley dropped back onto the sidewalk with a loud thump and a little yelp of pain.

Claudia had been standing in the open door of the home. She had been knocked backward, but managed to hang onto the second antitank missile as she fell.

McCallum quickly scrambled back up, knelt on the sidewalk, and aimed the antitank launcher upward again. "Claudia! Another missile!"

She was already headed his way.

Now he could see the blackness move slowly against the background of stars. A soft red spot seemed to glow in the center of it, maybe from where the missile had hit. But it was still up there. The missile hadn't done much to it, it seemed.

Claudia handed him the second missile and he loaded it into place.

"Brace yourselves," he shouted to the others.

Beside him Claudia dropped to the grass.

The blackness drifted to the side and down slightly, smashing with a loud crashing sound into the tops of the nearby pine trees before climbing up again.

"Maybe I did do some damage," McCallum said. "How about I do some more?"

The black shape drifted away from the pine trees and seemingly up higher.

McCallum aimed at the red spot. "Here we go again!" he shouted, took a deep breath, and fired again.

He was rocked backward as the missile shot away.

This missile took only an instant longer than the first to reach its target.

Again an explosion lit up the night and the strange shapes on the underside of the craft. The craft was like nothing McCallum had ever seen outside a science fiction movie. Round, black, and very large.

An instant later the blast impact smashed into him and knocked him tumbling backward into the grass.

He sat up quickly as the huge black shape, now with two glowing spots, side by side, moved up and up, hovered for a moment, then shot off toward the eastern mountains.

McCallum climbed to his feet and turned to Claudia, who still sat on the grass. "You all right?" he managed to ask, his voice shaky.

"I think so."

McCallum offered her a hand up and she took it. And then hugged him as she got upright.

The three guardsmen also seemed to be climbing to their feet. And inside the resident center lights were coming on and alarms were sounding. McCallum could see a dozen windows broken out along the front of the building. In a few minutes this place was going to be a zoo of police, fire engines, and reporters.

"Mr. Ashley!" Claudia shouted. She let go of McCallum and ran down the sidewalk to where the old man lay, moaning. A leg was twisted back up under him, obviously broken.

"What exactly was that?" one of the guardsmen asked, his voice trembling as he stared at the night sky.

McCallum laughed. "As a person once said to me, you wouldn't believe me if I told you."

32

If there was no such thing as coincidence, there would be no such word.

—HERON CARVIC
FROM *PICTURE MISS SEETON*

1:45 A.M. JUNE 26.
WASHINGTON, D.C.

The president of the United States pulled his thick brown robe tightly around himself as he entered the Oval Office. He'd been awakened by a phone call from the vice president, who had been awake overseeing the coming search of the nation's cities. In John's few years at this job he'd only been awakened twice before, and neither time was good news. He didn't expect this to be, either.

Vice President Alan Wallace was pacing when John entered. He was dressed in the same suit as earlier in the day, but his tie had somehow vanished and his hair hadn't seen a comb since lunch.

As John closed the door from his private office, Alan said, "Sorry to wake you, sir."

John waved him off and went to the tray of coffee and juice the staff had managed to get in place. "Just tell me what's happened."

"It's Portland again, sir."

John spun around, spilling some of the orange juice from the small pitcher. "Christ, it's still there, isn't it?"

"Yes, sir," Alan said. "Sorry to startle you."

The president snorted, a habit he'd only picked up in the last year, mostly while listening to things he didn't want to respond to. "Just get to the problem."

"The Portland mayor and police, with the help of the National Guard, set up stakeouts at nursing homes and retirement centers around their city this evening. They figured the Klar might try to get another elderly man for taking a bomb into Portland. They were right."

"So another poor soul has been abducted, huh?"

"No, sir," Alan said. "They stopped it. Richard McCallum, the man who found the first bomb, and a few national guardsmen had a run-in with a Klar ship as it tried the abduction from a secluded retirement home."

"What?" John said. He'd managed to get about half a glass of orange juice drunk. "Run-in? What in hell's name did they do? And did they really see an alien ship?"

"They saw one, sir," Alan said. "They stopped a man from being lifted into it."

"How did they manage to do that?"

"McCallum hit the Klar ship with two antitank missiles."

The president set his glass down, walked around behind his desk and slumped into his chair. "I'm afraid to ask," he said, slowly. "Did he down it?"

Alan shook his head no. "I wish. But he did manage, it seems, to do some damage. The thing smashed the tops off about thirty pine trees trying to get away."

"So the Foster report may be correct. These aliens might not be that far ahead of us in technology, that is, if we can dent one with an antitank missile."

"We don't know, sir," the vice president said. "But two antitank missiles didn't down it."

John sat thinking for a moment. "Is this going to hurt the bomb search tomorrow in any way?"

"I don't think so, sir. And neither does Neda Foster. Everything is almost ready. But the press in Portland are going nuts. I guess the shots McCallum fired could be seen all over the city."

"Stonewall them," John said, flatly. "Nothing until after the search. Nothing. I want any chance of panic over those bombs being in the cities stopped cold. Understand? No reporting, no panic."

"Yes, sir," Alan said.

Again there was silence between them for a moment, then the president said, "McCallum. Who is this guy?"

"An ex-cop turned private investigator," Alan said. "I met him. Seems sharp."

John nodded. "Found the first bomb. And now fired the first shot in what may turn out to be the first true World War. I'm just glad he's on our side."

"So am I, sir," Alan said.

The president waved him toward the door. "I want a full report of what happened in Portland on my desk as soon as it comes in. Now go back to work. It seems I have a few dozen phone calls to make again."

The vice president nodded and turned for the door.

"Oh, Alan," John said.

Alan turned. "Yes, sir."

John smiled. "You know that meeting with the Joint Chiefs we talked about? Better schedule it for the war room tomorrow evening, after the bomb searches are over for the day. We've got some explaining to do, I'm sure. And plans to make."

"I'll schedule it, sir," Alan said, smiling at the president. Then, as he turned away, he said, "But I won't look forward to it."

33

Digestion should be considered before *a meal.*

—VICTOR WHITECHURCH
FROM *THRILLING STORIES OF THE RAILWAY*

2:15 A.M. JUNE 26.
PORTLAND, OREGON

The mayor sat behind her desk, her hair pulled back into a tight ponytail, the phone against her ear. She wore a baggy knit sweater and old jeans. Circles were slowly starting to form under her eyes. For a good two minutes, since the phone rang, she hadn't said more than two words.

McCallum sat in an overstuffed armchair to her right, against the bookcases. Claudia sat on the arm of his chair, resting her hand on his shoulder. Her hand felt good there and every so often he reached up and squeezed it.

Regional FBI Director Earhart had taken the chair directly in front of Janet's desk and the Portland chief of police had the one beside him.

Henry stood against the bookcases on the left.

Both Earhart and the chief of police were dressed as if they had tossed on whatever was closest when called out of bed. On an end table beside Henry was a box of doughnuts. Henry said he had brought them for everyone, but he was the only one eating them.

They were all waiting silently for Janet to get off the phone. They all knew it was an important call.

Over the last half hour, before the phone call, they had gone over exactly what had occurred on that hill tonight, detail by detail. McCallum still couldn't believe he had actually seen a Klar ship, let alone fired at one. Images of those statues of the Klar in Neda Foster's lab kept floating through his mind, no matter how hard he tried to keep them out.

But there was something bothering McCallum much, much more. About an hour after the encounter with the ship, Henry had slapped him on the shoulder and said, "Congratulations, you almost shot down a UFO."

He meant it jokingly. McCallum was sure of that. But McCallum felt his knees get weak and he couldn't even think of a response to Henry.

"Yes, sir," the mayor said into the phone. "I understand. Thank you."

She waited another moment and then hung up.

After a deep breath, she looked up at those around her. "Okay, people, as some of you might have guessed, that was the vice president."

McCallum thought it might have been. It seemed that Alan Wallace was taking the lead position on all this. And from what McCallum had seen of him, that was a good thing. The guy had the ability to get things done when they needed to be done. And right now they *really* needed to be done.

"Two things," Janet said, "that we have to get worked out tonight before any of us can try to get to sleep. First, we need to be ready to search the city again tomorrow just as every other city in the country is being searched."

"Why?" Henry said. "We found our bomb, and so far tonight we've kept them from taking another carrier pigeon."

Henry had started calling the thing-on-the-bed a carrier pigeon. McCallum was glad that so far no one else had taken up his slang.

"Neda Foster's organization is sending down pictures of elderly abductees from Seattle, the Tri-Cities, and Boise. We're not taking any chances that one of them might be here, carrying another bomb. We'll do the search. And we'll do it right."

Everyone in the room agreed with her.

"Mr. Earhart, could you work with the police to get this set up?"

"Of course, Mayor," he said. "It's already being done."

Beside him the chief of police nodded. "We'll be ready for an eight A.M. start, right with the rest of the country."

"Good," Janet said. "Thank you. Now to item number two: the Press."

McCallum could feel Claudia stiffen beside him. Normally that would be her job, but she had been personally involved tonight. She wasn't the right person to do that job.

"The vice president said we must keep a tight lid on what really happened on that hill tonight," Janet said. "Are those three national guardsmen under wraps?"

Earhart nodded. "They've been flown to Seattle for debriefing. They will be there for days at least."

"And Mr. Ashley?"

"He's in the hospital," Henry said. "He doesn't know what hit him. And he saw nothing."

"Okay," Janet said. "So I'm going into that press conference in a moment and tell them the truth without telling them anything."

McCallum sat up a little. "Mayor, could you tell us first, what you're going to say, so we all have our stories straight?"

McCallum was convinced that the press had to stay out of this for at least the next few days. If they spread the bomb scare over the front pages of every newspaper, the panic and looting would kill thousands. And it also might push the Klar into setting off the bombs already planted. So as far as McCallum was concerned, at this moment the American press was the biggest threat there was outside the Klar. And thanks to him blasting that ship, it was falling on the mayor of Portland to be the front line of defense.

Janet nodded. "The vice president said to tell them we had two explosions. Everyone saw those."

"Some a little closer than others," McCallum said, and Henry actually laughed.

"I'm going to tell them that we have no leads on the source of the explosions, but a full investigation is underway. I'm going to tell them the FBI is involved. And that's about it."

No one had anything to add, so Janet glanced at her watch. "We have less than six hours until we start the search. Let's get moving."

McCallum pushed himself to his feet as Janet did the same thing.

Henry grabbed the box of doughnuts and tucked them under his arm.

The chief of police and FBI Regional Director Earhart started talking as they headed toward the door.

"One more thing," Janet called out before the door was open.

McCallum, with his hand in Claudia's, stopped and turned to the mayor along with the rest of them.

Janet turned to McCallum. "Richard, officially, for the city and its people, I want to thank you for what you did yesterday and tonight. I wish I could do it in a more public way, but it seems I can't."

Claudia squeezed his hand.

McCallum smiled at Janet. "Coming from you, Mayor, this is more than enough. Thank you."

"Wait until you get his bill," Henry said.

And everyone laughed as the mayor led the way to the pressroom.

34

When all are prisoners, the jailers are free men.

—TED ALLBEURY
FROM *SHADOW OF SHADOWS*

5:51 A.M. JUNE 26.
SHEEPEATER CAVES, EASTERN OREGON

"I think we're getting close," Cobb said, his voice muffled by the rock and dirt around him. In the opening in front of her, Tina Harris could faintly see Cobb's feet as he inched himself forward into the hole they'd been working on.

Above her the morning light was coming through the crack in the roof, giving fair warning of another long day of heat. And, unless the aliens brought water and food, it might be her last.

Around her, others lay scattered around the cave. The older man who had first talked to her appeared to be dead, his body covered with black flies. His skin seemed to be moving by itself, and she watched in distant horror for a moment.

The two women with him weren't in much better shape. They lay side by side, not moving except for an occasional rise and fall from breathing. They wouldn't make it through the heat of another day.

Tina was the only person in the room standing. And, besides Cobb, most likely the only person who still could.

She glanced down at the hole where she could see Cobb's feet. What Cobb had thought would only take an hour, to open the passage into the next area of cave, had taken most of the night. And it still wasn't totally open yet, even though they'd both taken turns working on it since before the sun went down. There had just been too many big rocks they had to dig out.

Tina knelt and put her head into the hole. "It's starting to get light," she said.

"Damn," she heard him say, his voice distant and muffled by the dirt and rocks.

After a moment he started to inch backward.

She stood and waited for him, not even having the energy to help him out. A half minute later he stood up and pretended to brush some of the dirt off his hands. But it was only a remembered motion from the past and did no good. His hands were as cut and bleeding as Tina's. And every inch of his body was streaked black with dirt and covered with scrapes.

"It's so close," he said, his voice tired. "So close."

"Tonight," she said. But she could tell her voice had no belief in it either. "We'll make it tonight, if there is anywhere to make it to in there."

"I'm sure there is," Cobb said. "I can feel the fresh air

hitting my face. You felt it too, you said. That means there's another way out. It has to."

Or just a crack in the ceiling of another small cave, Tina thought, but didn't say out loud.

Cobb glanced around his feet as the light in the cave suddenly became brighter. The sun must have crested a hill to the east, shining directly on the crack above. Soon the cave would start heating up.

Dirt and rocks from their night of work littered the area around the small opening they had created. "We need to hide this," Cobb said.

Tina almost asked what difference it would make, then bent down and started pushing dirt to one side. After a few minutes they had most of the dirt down in cracks between larger rocks and the smaller rocks scattered around the area. They rolled a big boulder over to block most of the hole, then they both sat down on the ground against it, using their bodies to cover some of the area of work.

Tina was beyond exhaustion. She couldn't even feel her feet and legs anymore and the cave around her already felt hot.

"I need to sleep," Tina said, slumping down with her feet out in front of her.

"I'll be right behind you," Cobb said, doing the same beside her.

She let her head rest against his shoulder and almost instantly she was asleep, dreaming of Jerry.

And of dark caves.

And hot, hot summer days without relief.

35

Who feeds on hope alone makes but a sorry banquet.

—THOMAS W. HANSHEW
FROM *CLEEK, THE MAN OF THE FORTY FACES*

12:42 P.M. JUNE 26.
WASHINGTON, D.C.

The president of the United States couldn't stand another minute on the phone. The search for bombs in American cities had been going on now for almost two hours. Around the world there had already been eighteen hydrogen bombs found that he knew of, all of which had been disarmed. He was far beyond thinking that there wouldn't be any more bombs in American cities. Now the only question was how the search was going. And if he had made the right decision, running it the way they were.

So far this morning he'd forced himself to stay in his office, out of the way, and call the leaders of other countries, letting Alan run the search. But now he couldn't stand it anymore. He had to know what was happening.

He strode through his private office and into the hall. A few strides later he was in the vice president's office. FBI Director Barns sat at a table, his jacket off and his sleeves rolled up, typing into a laptop computer plugged into a phone line. He glanced at John and nodded, but didn't stop typing.

Alan sat behind his desk, a phone against his ear. He also nodded to John, then pointed to the wall.

On the wall opposite the door, the vice president's pictures of his hometown had been taken down and a huge map of the United States had been tacked up.

John moved over in front of it. On the map were nineteen green pins stuck in cities. Almost all the cities were the smaller ones. There was still no pin in New York, Chicago, Los Angeles, or San Francisco.

"Thanks," Alan said. "Good work." He hung up the phone, grabbed another green pin and came around the desk.

"Green means clean cities, or bombs found?" John asked.

"Bombs found," Alan said. He stuck the pin in Boston. "That makes twenty."

The president dropped down into an armchair. "My God," he said. "Are we doing this right? Should we be running this out of the war room, with the full army involved? This is a huge attack on our country."

Alan moved back over behind his desk and dropped into his chair. "Sir, with the army involved, we'd have set off a panic that would have cost thousands of lives and billions of dollars in damage. A panic we might never have recovered from."

John nodded. He had used the same argument earlier. But he was having trouble remembering it.

"As it is," Alan went on, "so far the press are baffled as to what's happening. There is no panic. And with only local police and FBI involved, we're finding the bombs. We may decide to get the army involved with the next step, tonight, at the meeting with the Joint Chiefs."

John looked at Alan. He was right and John knew it. But a paper map tacked on a wall instead of the big computers in the war room? It just spooked him, made him feel as if they were running a partial operation when a full-scale one was needed and called for.

But the full-scale operation would come into play once the cities were safe. Once that was the case they had to keep them that way.

The phone rang again and Alan picked it up with only a curt "Yes."

After a moment he said, "Great," and hung up. He smiled at John, grabbed two more pins, and moved around to the map. He stuck one into New York City and the other into Washington, D.C. Then he turned and said, "We're safe for the time being."

John stared at that green pin sticking in Washington for a moment, then started laughing. It had not occurred to him at any point that he should leave the White House. His place was here. The thought of danger had not really crossed his mind when he knew he had a job to do. If the Secret Service knew what he and Alan had just done, by both staying here, they would throw a massive fit.

"I guess we're a little more alike than I thought," the president said, still chuckling to himself, thinking of how he'd chewed Alan out for doing basically what he had just done.

Alan laughed as the phone rang again. "Maybe that's why you picked me as your running mate in the first place."

"Maybe it was," the president said as Alan grabbed the phone, listened for a few seconds and then picked up three more green pins.

36

There are always exceptions to every rule, but only if you really know what you're doing.

—ELIZABETH PETERS
FROM *DIE FOR LOVE*

12:58 P.M. JUNE 26.
PORTLAND, OREGON

McCallum sat in Binky's Doughnuts off Front Street. The place was Henry's favorite doughnut shop in the entire city, and one day he hoped to either buy it or start one of his own. It had orange plastic seats, plastic plants, and bright fluorescent lights. McCallum hated the doughnuts, but had to admit it had good, basic coffee, not that Seattle stuff. Henry had bought a half dozen doughnuts and two coffees, dropped them at the table, and then went to call in. At the moment there was no one else in the place besides the teenage girl behind the counter.

McCallum sipped on his coffee and thought about the events of the day while Henry talked on the phone near the cash register. The search of the Portland area had turned up nothing, and was pretty much winding down. The *Oregonian* this morning had called his missile shots in the western hills "Unexplained Explosions." And had no real details.

At lunch not one word had come out over the national news services about alien attacks, hydrogen bombs, or massive manhunts in the core of every city.

Nothing. Not one word.

So far they were pulling this off.

From what the mayor had told him thirty minutes ago, the vice president said they were finding the bombs in every city. She had said that in each city they were sealing off the room the bomb and thing-on-the-bed was found in, and then bringing in a special elite crew from the FBI to deal with each one. That kept the number of people involved down to a very few, even though there were thousands helping in the manhunts.

McCallum took a sip of coffee, amazed that this could even happen in an instant-news society. It made him wonder what else had happened over the years that the general public hadn't heard about.

Henry hung up the phone and came back over to their table, smiling as he wound his thick bulk through the maze of orange plastic chairs.

"The mayor just held a news conference," he said, grabbing a doughnut and talking between bites. "She told them that the search of the downtown area this morning was for people possibly associated with the blasts in the western hills last night. That nothing was found, and there are no new leads. She's smooth, huh?"

"That she is," McCallum said. "But what happens tonight? And tomorrow night? Are we going to just keep staking out nursing homes with antitank weapons? We're missing something here that I just can't put my finger on. Something we need to be doing and aren't."

Henry shrugged. "Can't tell you what it is, old partner." He washed down the doughnut with a full gulp of his coffee, then grabbed another white-frosted doughnut, holding it up to stare at. "Amazing how this guy manages to get these so perfect."

As Henry took a bite of the doughnut McCallum reached over and picked up another doughnut from the box, staring at it. Something about the doughnut seemed to tie into all this.

The saucer he saw was round, but that wasn't it. There was something else. Then he remember Henry's words about radius the day before.

And last night the Klar ship, when hit, had gone east, not up into space.

Radius.

Neda Foster's group had been assuming that the Klar would put the abducted elderly people back in the same city they were taken from. And the assumption had been right. Which meant the Klar ships were staying close to certain areas.

Why would the Klar do that? The answer to that question was the solution to slowing down the Klar even more than they already had been.

"Thought you didn't like those," Henry said, pointing to the doughnut in McCallum's hand.

"I don't. But I do like the shape," McCallum said, dropping the doughnut back into the box, standing, and turning for the phone near the counter. "Better order some more," he called out to Henry. "We're heading for Bellingham again."

"You know," Henry called out, "sleep would be nice someday."

McCallum agreed. But the flight to Bellingham on the Harris jet wasn't even long enough to take a nap.

37

How can anyone decide whether a given fact is important or not unless one knows everything about it—and no one knows everything about anything.

—FREDRIC BROWN
FROM *NIGHT OF THE JABBERWOCK*

1:47 P.M. JUNE 26.
BELLINGHAM, WASHINGTON

Neda Foster sat at her desk. She felt sticky with sweat and grime, and the taste in her mouth was of one too many cups of coffee. She couldn't remember the last time she had slept. The Klar attacking the cities had all happened too fast, and in such an odd way. Never had anyone in her organization thought that the Klar would plant bombs in the cities.

Never.

And never had she expected anyone to fire on a Klar ship. Now the president and vice president were involved and the fight was going beyond this lab. That thought made her sad and at the same time very relieved.

Cornell dropped down into the chair facing her desk.

"They're an organic constructed shell with a miniaturized computer to run them," he said, assuming Neda knew that *they* meant the things-on-the-bed. "An acid substance fills tubes throughout their bodies."

"They're robots?" Neda said, letting the shock fill her question as the doctor's words sank into her tired mind.

"Basically, yes," Cornell said. "Organic robots. My guess is the face and outside are formed by pouring an organic substance over the model, like a mold, then forming the finished product around a form of plastic skeleton, run by small motors controlled by a small computer."

"And the voice?"

Cornell shrugged. "Easy," he said. "Recorded and digitized. We can do that now ourselves. Just a certain number of voice tracks set to respond to certain things. A watch-sized computer could run the entire thing and most likely did."

"So why'd it melt?"

Cornell smiled. "That's the interesting part," he said. "They filled the entire body with tubes of acid, and when the program was short-circuited, the acid flooded the inside of the body, melting the entire thing into a pool, destroying all evidence."

"Standard Klar conservatism," Neda said. "They were still afraid of being discovered right up until they thought we could no longer stop them."

"Sure seems that way," Cornell said. "But now that we spotted their elderly carriers and stopped that, they can shift to having anyone carry those bombs into the cities. I figure they can make these robot-things in about a day's time. And heaven only knows how many bombs they can make."

The tiredness overwhelmed her. Somehow there had to

be a way of stopping the Klar. Otherwise they'd be fighting this underground war against bombs for years and years, with the Klar ultimately winning.

The phone rang on her desk and she managed to pick it up, even though her arms felt like lead.

"Neda," the voice said. "This is Alan Wallace."

She sat up straight. She'd talked to the vice president just a few hours ago, and the search had been going fine. Had something gone wrong? "Yes, sir," she said. "Alan, I mean."

He laughed, but she could tell, even over the phone, that his laugh was a tired one. "Just wanted to tell you that we've found and disarmed the bombs in every major city but Los Angeles and Dallas. And the searches are continuing there."

"Great to hear," she said, relief flooding through her, making her seem even more tired, if that was possible.

"Also," he said, "as of this hour eighty-four bombs have been found in other countries. And many more searches are still happening, especially in China, Japan, and Australia."

"Wonderful," she said.

"So, for the moment," Alan said, "we seem to be past the crisis. Is that what your group feels, also?"

"Yes, it is," Neda said. "The Klar are far too careful to try anything now, with most of the bombs gone. But sir, they will keep going. They won't stop. Dr. Cornell has figured out how the things-on-the-bed were made, and we think the Klar will just start using regular people as patterns. Anyone they can abduct."

There was a long pause on the other end of the line, then Alan said, "We were afraid of just that. Which brings me to my second question. We're leaning toward keeping this completely silent, as much as possible. And denying anything that does leak out. Do you agree?"

Neda glanced at the tired-looking Dr. Cornell, then said, "Yes, sir, I think that's critical."

"And why's that?"

Neda laughed. "About a thousand reasons. But first is that the press will hang you and your boss out to dry, even though you saved the world today."

"True," he said.

"Sir," she said, very bluntly, "we need you where you are for the moment."

"Okay," Alan said. "I won't argue that point. What's the second of the thousand reasons?"

"A double-sided point," Neda said, forcing herself to sit up straight and clear the tiredness from her mind by sheer will. What she said now might affect how the entire fight against the Klar went for years to come. "First off, millions will not believe aliens are really here. Bombs or no bombs, we have no real proof."

"True," Alan said.

"Just read any tabloid," Neda continued, "or watch any science fiction movie to see how aliens are thought of in this world. They don't exist because we as humans can't have them exist. We humans must be the center of the universe."

"Agreed," Alan said.

"And if you tell the public about the hydrogen bombs in the cities, and that there might be more at any time, you'll start a panic that will kill millions. The cities will become ghost towns, and the Klar will be on their way to winning that way."

Again there was silence on the other end of the line for

a long time. Finally the vice president said, "That's exactly the conclusion the president and I had come to. We're going into a meeting with the Joint Chiefs in a few hours. We've decided we're going to keep them in the dark for now. I just wanted to run that past you."

"I think that's for the better," Neda said. "But what did the president tell all the foreign heads of state? How'd he get them to search without telling them about aliens?"

Alan laughed. "He said nothing about aliens. He figured they'd all have hung up on him. He told them he had knowledge of a sophisticated terrorist group planting bombs in cities. He told each to keep it very quiet, and had, in all but five cases, special CIA two-man teams take care of the carrier and the bomb once they were found."

"Amazing," Neda said. "So very few people actually know about the bombs. And even fewer know about the Klar?"

"That's correct," Alan said. "It is amazing."

"And the press?"

"We're giving them nothing. And if they press it too hard, or discover anything about the Klar, they'll look like the tabloids and no one will believe them."

"Nice," Neda said. She was massively relieved.

"Look," Alan said, "over the next few days the president and I will be setting up a very secret group to deal with this threat. We want to work with your group as much as possible."

"That would be fine with us," she said. "The more the merrier, as the old saying goes."

The vice president laughed. "I'll agree with you on that. I'll be in touch."

And with that he hung up.

Neda dropped the phone into its place and looked up at

Cornell. "It seems we're still in the undercover alien-chasing business."

"Good," Cornell said. "I think where the Klar are concerned, it's safer for everyone that way."

Neda glanced around at the two huge statues towering over her and could only agree.

38

When you have a bee in your bonnet, you don't start swinging a fly swatter.

—MICHAEL AVALLONE
FROM *THE TALL DELORES*

2:19 P.M. JUNE 26.
BELLINGHAM, WASHINGTON

McCallum and Henry walked into Neda Foster's Bellingham lab and were shown inside immediately. No waiting around in the outside room this time. McCallum had called from the Harris jet and told Neda he had an idea and was on his way. She had just gotten off the phone with the vice president, so she filled him in on what was happening and the president's decision to keep everything quiet.

McCallum found on hearing that news that he was very, very relieved. For some reason the thought of having his picture plastered all over the tabloids as the first human to ever fire a weapon at an alien ship didn't please him.

Inside the lab the two statues of the Klar stopped both him and Henry cold again. McCallum doubted he would ever get used to seeing them. The two monsters seemed to be staring down at him with their snake eyes. It made his skin crawl.

"Think maybe you made them mad last night?" Henry whispered.

"Maybe," McCallum said. He gave the two statues one long look and then headed for where Neda Foster waited at her desk. Dr. Cornell waited with her.

"Nice shooting last night," Cornell said. "I've been wanting to ask you what reaction you saw when the antitank missiles hit their ship. It might help us figure out what the things are made of."

"I'll be glad to give you a detailed account," McCallum said. "But first there's an idea I want to run past you folks."

Neda indicated two chairs, but McCallum instead pointed at the world map that filled a large chunk of the center of the room. "Can we talk there?"

Neda shrugged, and all four of them moved over to the map.

"First off," McCallum said, "I need to get myself up to speed on some basics. The Klar abducted elderly men and then planted something that looked like them back in the same cities. How did you folks come to the correct assumption they'd do that when you came to Portland for that first search?"

Neda frowned, glanced at Cornell, then faced McCallum. "Years of pattern research," Neda said. "The Klar are very, very conservative in their actions. We think that's due to a number of factors. First, they've been in hiding on this planet for a long, long time. Second, they have very few resources of their own. They brought very few ships."

"And that helped you figure all that out?" Henry asked. "Amazing amount of detective work."

"That," Neda said, "and a wild amount of luck. But from what we know of the Klar, they tend to stay within certain habits. Planting the same person back in the same town would only seem logical to them."

"I remember you saying a maximum of twenty ships," McCallum said. "How did you come up with that number?"

"Again, simply observation and research from data collected over a lot of years," Neda said. "And also the laws of physics and economics. We have four space shuttles in NASA. Imagine how small an expenditure that would be compared to building twenty interstellar ships the size of the Klar ships. So from that starting point we knew they had very few ships. From other data, we have come to the number twenty."

"Give or take one," Dr. Cornell said.

"Okay," McCallum said. "You folks were very, very right about the elderly in the cities, so I'll accept your theory on twenty ships." McCallum turned to the huge world map. "So, does each Klar ship have a certain area of the planet it covers?"

"You mean like a salesman's territory?" Henry said.

"It seems that way," Neda said. "Their ships do have distinctively different marks, and what few sightings there are always have the same ships in the same areas of the world."

"So where are they based?" McCallum said. "Or do they go back into space every day?"

Cornell really laughed at that comment. "It would take a huge amount of resources for ships that size to constantly break out of the gravity well of Earth. And in space there would be a much higher chance they would be detected. No, they stay near the surface and move at night. Where, exactly, is another matter."

"Radius," McCallum said softly to himself.

"What are you getting at?" Neda Foster asked.

"When he gets like this," Henry said, "it means he has an idea. I've learned over the years to just stand back."

McCallum stared at the map with all the pins stuck in it, then turned to Neda Foster. "Can you tell me what area you think the Klar ship for this part of the world covers?"

Neda nodded. "We think the ship you shot at covers an area from Alaska down the coast to northern California above San Francisco. And inland to western Montana, all of Idaho, Washington, the western Canadian provinces, and northern Arizona."

"Wow," Henry said. "That's some territory."

"You got a pin and some string?" McCallum asked.

Neda nodded, turned, and rummaged through a desk drawer until she came up with some twine. As she handed it to him she said, "I wish you'd fill us in on what you are doing."

"I'm trying to figure out just where the Klar ships are," he said.

"We've been trying to do that for five years," Cornell said.

"Can I climb into the map there?" McCallum asked, pointing to the trap door in the ocean off the coast of the Pacific northwest.

"Be my guest," Neda said.

McCallum ducked down and went under the wood platform structure of the map the eight feet to the right spot, then slowly pushed up the trapdoor.

"A monster rising out of the ocean," Henry said as McCallum stood up. "Godzilla needed a mate last time I checked."

"Claudia would be jealous," McCallum said, as he quickly went to work. He stretched the string from the lower part of Alaska to just above San Francisco and cut it with his pocket knife.

Then he folded it in half and marked the halfway spot. It ended up just south of Portland. He laid another piece of the string down on the map from that spot straight inland from west to east.

"Radius," Cornell said. "I follow where you're going. You think the Klar might have their bases near the center of each ship's territory?"

"From what you've told me about how conservative with resources they are, wouldn't that make sense?"

"It most certainly would," Neda Foster said, leaning over the map to see better.

McCallum ran his finger on the string he had laid out west to east on the map. "The center of the two extreme north-south edges of their area runs from below Portland in the west, over the center part of Idaho and northern Yellowstone Park."

"That's still a lot of rough country," Henry said.

McCallum nodded. It was. And he was beginning to feel as if his idea might not work.

"Okay," Dr. Cornell said. "Let's see if we can shorten that line by taking the radius east to west. Take your same measuring string and mark off from the coast inland."

McCallum did as the doctor suggested, and the end of the string landed on the border of Montana and Idaho.

"Too far," Neda said. "We're fairly convinced this ship doesn't go farther inland than the continental divide."

"I'll measure from Butte, Montana to the coast and cut that in half."

"Logical," Cornell said. "Crude, but logical."

McCallum took another piece of string, measured the distance, folded the string in half and then laid it down from the coast inland. The end of the string landed right near Hells Canyon, on the border between Idaho and Oregon. Some of the most remote, least populated country in the lower forty-eight states.

"Hells Canyon area," Cornell said to himself.

"Nasty country," Henry said.

McCallum ducked down and scrambled out from the middle of the map. As he came out, Cornell was already headed for a nearby computer.

Neda indicated that they should follow him.

"The Klar ships are a certain size," the doctor said. "And it would take a certain size natural formation to hide one. We also believe they hide in deep forest, jungle, and possibly even buildings made to look like factories. But there are very few deep, thick forests, jungles, or huge buildings in the Hells Canyon area."

So what are you looking for?" Henry asked.

"Caves, Detective," Cornell said. "More precisely, a cave with a large enough entrance to hide a Klar ship. I've given the computer the parameters and told it to search the geologic records of the area on both sides of Hells Canyon in a hundred mile radius for any likely sites."

After a moment the computer stopped its search. "Three places," Cornell said, reading the screen. "First are the Higby Caves, east of Boise. They're smack between the air-force base in Boise and the one in Mountain Home. The Klar would never use it."

"One down," Henry said.

"Another is right above Idaho State Highway 95, and is an open tourist attraction."

"Two down," Henry said.

"The third," the doctor said, "is in an isolated canyon in the high Oregon desert. An old Indian cave called the Sheepeater Caves."

"Bingo," Henry said.

Neda turned and stared at the big map for a moment, then looked over at McCallum with a very serious expression on her face. "You want another shot at that ship?"

"If I have a bigger gun," he said. Actually he didn't want to get near a Klar ship again, but he had no choice at this point. It seemed he was in this fight whether he wanted to be or not.

Neda laughed. "I can arrange that," she said.

She moved over and picked up the phone on her desk, punched in a series of numbers, and after a moment said, "I'd like to talk to the vice president."

"Now you've done it," Henry said to McCallum.

"Seems that way," McCallum said, glancing up at the two Klar statues staring at him.

"Okay," Cornell said, sounding more like a kid with a

new toy than a scientist, "using that same crude method, let's see if we can find some more ships. Climb into the trapdoor in the Gulf of Mexico."

"Yeah," Henry said, smiling at McCallum. "And this time try not to get wet."

39

It is a rare mind indeed that can render the hitherto nonexistent blindingly obvious.

—DOUGLAS ADAMS
FROM *DIRK GENTLY'S HOLISTIC DETECTIVE AGENCY*

5:32 P.M. JUNE 26.
WASHINGTON, D.C.

The vice president knocked and entered the Oval Office. Inside, the president was sitting on the couch across from his personal secretary and his chief of staff, Dan Follet. Dan, who knew something was going on, but whom the president had excluded for the time being, gave Alan a dirty look.

"Problem, Alan?" John asked immediately when he saw the vice president.

"Something that needs to be discussed, sir," Alan said. He'd just gotten off the phone with Neda Foster and her request had stunned him. But if there was a chance she and her people, including McCallum, were correct, quick action might save some lives and shut down the Klar for the immediate future.

John excused himself from the others and nodded that Alan should follow him into his private office. Alan could feel the chief of staff's gaze boring into his back and it made him smile. He'd never liked the guy anyway.

After the door was closed behind them, Alan said, "I just spoke to Neda Foster. McCallum is there and has come up with a lead that might allow us to find where the Klar ships hide during the day."

"McCallum again," John said, shaking his head in disbelief. "So did they find a ship?"

"That's the problem, sir," Alan said. "Neda asked that the location be approached by at least three army attack helicopters, fully armed and ready to fight. She said that if there is a ship there, they might as well try to take it out. Her words, sir."

"Damn," John said, sitting down behind his desk. He stared at the top of the desk for a moment, then looked up. "When?"

"As soon as possible," Alan said. "They'd like to go in before dark. Try to stop more abductions and keep bombs from being planted in the cities."

John nodded. "Did she say what part of the world this ship might be in?"

"Eastern Oregon," Alan said.

"Well, at least it's in this country." The president picked up his phone and said, "Get me General Hoffman. Emergency."

While he was waiting, he glanced up at Alan. "Tell Miss Foster that General Hoffman will be in contact with her and that she should be ready to go within the hour. There'll be four ships. One will carry her and whoever she chooses to take along and will stay back out of the action."

"I'll tell her, sir," Alan said, turning and heading for the door.

Behind him he heard the president mutter, "That woman's going to get me impeached yet."

40

Authentic detail can always be used to beef up unsubstantiated theory.

—ROSS THOMAS
FROM *IF YOU CAN'T BE GOOD*

3:47 P.M. JUNE 26.
BELLINGHAM, WASHINGTON

From the moment Neda Foster first called the vice president until General Hoffman walked through the door, McCallum and Henry, with Dr. Cornell on his computer, located three possible other sights for Klar ships: one in Mexico, one in Eastern Canada, and one in South America. They'd been so engrossed in what they were doing they hadn't even heard the army helicopter land in a nearby parking lot.

McCallum watched as General Hoffman came through the door of Neda Foster's lab, took two steps, and stopped to stare at the two Klar statues. Those two statues were very, very effective. And McCallum prayed he'd never have to meet a real Klar face to face.

The general was a stocky man of fifty, with intense blue eyes, and white hair buzz-cut to army-private standards. He also had huge forearms, so obviously the guy still worked out regularly. Everything about him just screamed *regular army*. He even wore his "battle greens," with his hat tucked under a strap on his shoulder.

Neda let him stare at the Klar for a moment, then extended her hand. "General Hoffman. I'm Neda Foster."

The general seemed startled. He snapped slightly more upright and took Neda's hand. "Glad to meet you." His voice was deep and thick and fit his stocky form.

Neda led the general over to the map of the world and did introductions. McCallum knew the general would have a firm handshake and he was right. He did.

"All right," the general said. "The president has ordered me to mount up my four best crews, arm the birds, and get ready for a full top secret battle. And he told me you'd be riding along and giving me the target. Is that correct?"

Neda managed a smile, but it was clearly a nervous smile. "That's correct, General."

He shook his head. "The oddest thing I've ever been ordered to do," he said. "And if John and I didn't go way back, I'd have sworn he was going over the edge."

"I'm glad the president managed to convince you," Neda said. "Because this might be one of the biggest fights you've ever been in."

The general snorted. "Two tours of 'Nam and Desert Storm. You're going to have to go some."

"Well then, General," Neda said. "Let's hope I'm wrong. But I don't think I will be, after this is all said and done. Now, how much did the president tell you?"

"Just what I told you," the general said. He glanced at McCallum, then Henry and Dr. Cornell, as if wondering who all the nuts were. McCallum recognized the look. He'd given it a few times himself.

"Yesterday," Neda said, "armed hydrogen bombs were discovered in both Portland and Tucson."

"What!" the general almost shouted. "How can that be? I heard nothing about that. Who did it?"

"Very few people heard about it, General," Neda said, holding up her hand for him to stop. "And even fewer know that more armed hydrogen bombs were found today in a massive search of every major American city. And almost a hundred foreign cities."

The general laughed, a sharp barking kind of laugh that said he clearly didn't believe what she was saying.

She turned, picked up the phone, and dialed a number. "General Hoffman would like to speak to the president," she said, and then handed the phone to the general. "He's expecting this," she said, smiling.

The general slowly put the phone to his ear, never taking his eyes off Neda Foster's face.

McCallum was enjoying the entire event. And gaining even more respect for the strong, blond woman who ran this operation. Neda knew how to get people on her side. And how to get things done when she needed them done. McCallum was very glad she was on his side, because he couldn't imagine trying to fight her on anything. He wasn't sure he'd win.

The general said, "Yes, John, I'm at Miss Foster's lab. And she just told me a story about hydrogen bombs in the cities and—"

The general listened intently, nodding once in a while, then finally said, "I understand, sir. Thank you for the trust, sir."

Then the general hung up the phone and turned to face

Neda. His face had gone white and he had small drops of sweat on his forehead.

"So the president explained that very few people know what happened yesterday and today. And now you are one of those few."

The general nodded and swallowed.

"Okay, General," Neda said. "The things that planted those bombs look like those two statues over there."

"Aliens?" the general said.

"They are called Klar, General," Neda said, giving the guy no time to recover. "And around the world at this moment they have hidden about twenty ships. Mr. McCallum here actually hit one with two antitank missiles last night."

The general turned and looked at McCallum. "You saw one. Actually hit it?"

"Afraid so," McCallum said. "General, I didn't believe this three days ago either. But it's all true. Hydrogen bombs and all. These Klar things have attacked this country. They were within days of destroying our cities. It's now become our job to stop them."

McCallum knew that punching the general's *protect-the-nation* button would speed this process along. Behind the general, Neda smiled.

"That's what the president said," the general muttered. He took a deep breath, squared his shoulders, and looked at McCallum. "You hit it twice with antitank missiles. And you didn't bring it down?"

"No, sir," McCallum said. "But I dented it, and caused it to hit some trees before it recovered."

The general nodded. "Good. My birds carry a lot more punch than an antitank missile. We'll do more than dent the thing." He turned back to face Neda. "Where are we headed?"

"Eastern Oregon desert," Neda said. She indicated a large topographical map spread out on a nearby desk. "We need to plan this attack. We'll only have one chance, if we can surprise them during the daylight."

A moment later Henry, McCallum, Cornell, Neda, and the general were gathered around the map of Sheepeater Canyon, planning the attack.

41

As time passes we all get better at blazing a trail through the thicket of advice.

—MARGOT BENNETT
FROM *FAREWELL CROWN AND GOOD-BYE KING*

6:58 P.M. JUNE 26.
WASHINGTON, D.C.

Alan Wallace knocked lightly on the president's private office door.

"Come in," the president said.

Alan moved inside, closing the door behind him. "It's time, sir."

"Oh, joy," John said.

"Are you sure we shouldn't tell them more?"

John picked up a folder and tucked it under his arm as he stood. "No, I'm not. But would any of those men in there believe us?"

Alan had wondered that same thing. And he'd come to the same conclusion the president had obviously come to. At the moment there just wasn't enough to tell the Joint

Chiefs to overcome the huge mental jump from not believing in aliens to believing they are attacking the world.

"I suppose not, sir," Alan said.

"I'm going to tell them about the fact that a few hydrogen bombs were found in our cities, as well as other cities around the world. I'm *not* going to tell them how many. And I'm going to tell them the FBI and CIA are dealing with the problem as a terrorist problem, which, in truth, it is."

"And when they ask who's behind it?"

"I'm going to tell them a half-truth," John said. "I'm going to tell them we don't have enough information yet to be exactly sure. And then I'm going to stress the reasons we have to keep this out of the press."

"Sounds logical," Alan said. "I'm with you all the way."

"Thanks," John said. And Alan could tell he really meant it.

"Any news from Oregon?"

Alan shook his head. "They're in the air, headed for the location."

The president nodded. "So, as always, we wait."

"There is one thing Neda mentioned to me that we might need to deal with if they find a Klar ship where they're heading."

"And what's that?" John said, stopping short from opening his office door.

"They think they may know where three other ships might be."

"I figured they'd get that far," he said. "We'll deal with those possibilities after they see if they're right. Now, let's go put on a show for the Joint Chiefs."

"Right behind you, sir," Alan said, holding the door open.

"Someday, Alan," John said, "you might find yourself in this office, with people using that phrase with you. And you'll learn to hate it just as much as I do."

Alan grinned at the president. "Understood and noted, sir."

"Good," John said, chuckling. "Now walk beside me."

42

You need brains in this life of crime, but I often think you need luck even more.

—LESLIE CHARTERIS
FROM *THE SAINT IN "THE DAMSEL IN DISTRESS"*

4:25 P.M. JUNE 26.
EASTERN OREGON

The roar of the army attack helicopter was much more than a sound. It vibrated up through McCallum's body until it almost became part of him. With Henry and Neda Foster, he sat on the back bench seat on the right side. A young man in combat fatigues sat facing McCallum, checking over the machine gun mounted in the door. General Hoffman had the copilot's seat and a kid named Ron, who didn't look as though he could be much out of high school, flew the thing.

All of them had on headsets, with headphones that deadened the roar of the engines while allowing them to talk. But army helicopters were not made for comfort on any distance flight, so after the first few minutes the conversation had died down as they all just worked to survive the flight.

The plan they'd come up with back in Bellingham was simple. Fly high from Bellingham to a point near LaGrande, Oregon. Then drop down on the surface and go in fast. The big Sheepeater Cave was on the western face of the canyon, so they'd come in fast from the west over the desert, drop in over the mouth of the cave, and have the three attack helicopters take up positions over the far edge of the canyon with the command chopper above and behind them.

The worst part of the planning had come when the general asked Neda what kind of weapons they could expect in return and she said she didn't know. She said that, to her knowledge, the Klar had never fired a shot on Earth. At that point McCallum thought the general was going to call off the mission, Presidential order or not. And McCallum honestly couldn't blame the guy.

Far below them, the Columbia River cut a wide, blue path through the desert as the helicopter started a steep dive following the three others in formation ahead. "Almost there now," the general said. "Red Bluff One: Report."

McCallum could hear the voices of the other chopper pilots reporting status to the general as the four helicopters leveled out over desert sagebrush and skimmed along the surface at what seemed to be an extremely fast rate. McCallum had no way of judging and really didn't want to know how fast they were skimming over the rocks.

"Be ready for anything," the general said to his chopper crews. "You see a big, black ship of any configuration in that cave you are ordered to engage. We take it down and ask questions later. Understand?"

"Red Bluff One. Yes, sir."

"Red Bluff Two. Yes, sir."

"Red Bluff Three. Yes, sir."

"Good luck," the general said. He turned slightly and gave the three in the back seat a thumbs-up.

"McCallum," Henry said, "if we live though this I'm going to kill you."

McCallum patted Henry's leg and didn't answer. Both of them had seen plenty of action over the years. They'd gone through a lot of doors together. And been in their share of fights. But neither of them had military experience. And this was much, much closer than McCallum had ever wanted to get to combat, especially sitting in the back seat.

On the other side of Henry, Neda Foster's eyes seemed to be glazed over and she was continually licking her lips as she stared out the side door at the desert rushing past a few feet below. McCallum had no idea what she was thinking or feeling.

"Now!" the general shouted.

In a clearly practiced move, the young pilot took the helicopter up into a high arc. Below them a large rock canyon appeared in the desert floor.

Ron finished the arc upward and took the chopper around into a hard bank that slammed McCallum against the door.

"Someone needs to fix this rollercoaster," Henry said.

Ron brought the chopper to a sudden stop and tipped the nose of the chopper down at the canyon.

Over the general's shoulder McCallum could see a huge opening in the side of the rock-walled canyon. It looked like a lava cave. A small stream wound through the bottom of the canyon, surrounded by green brush and small trees. There was a dirt trail leading up to the cave mouth, but no other sign of occupation.

He could see no Klar ship.

The other three helicopters were stationed over the canyon rim across from the cave, all guns aimed at the hole.

Nothing happened.

They all waited. McCallum realized he was holding his breath.

Nothing.

McCallum forced himself to breathe.

"Red Bluff One. See anything in there?" the general demanded.

"Yes, I think so, sir. A large black shape back in the shadows. But there's no telling what it is."

"If it moves, take it out," the general said.

"Don't wait," both McCallum and Neda Foster shouted at the same moment, but it was too late.

An intense white beam shot out of the mouth of the cave, catching the center helicopter below them.

The pilot tried to pull away, but in less than a second the chopper exploded in a ball of orange flame.

"Fire!" the general yelled.

Instantly, missiles fired from the other two, smashing into the black shape as it started out of the cave.

McCallum watched as if the entire thing was in slow motion.

The ball of orange flame was still in the air where Red Bluff One had been. There didn't seem to be anything left at all of the helicopter or its crew.

Four missiles hit the emerging black shape almost instantly, sending a blast wave outward that rocked their helicopter, but Ron rode the blast like a pro cowboy, keeping the cave below them and in clear sight.

The black shape continued to come out of the cave like

a huge monster coming out of its hole. The missiles from the helicopters hadn't seemed to slow it down at all, just as McCallum's antitank missiles hadn't.

"Keep firing!" the general shouted, but he didn't need to. The other pilots were pulling back and continuing to fire. Two more missiles scored direct hits and the black thing seemed to disappear for a moment in a cloud of smoke and flame.

Then it was still there, almost out of the cave.

Still coming.

The thing was huge. Far larger than it seemed at night.

"Ron!" the general said to his pilot. "Fire half."

McCallum could feel the bumps of four rockets leaving the helicopter as Ron emptied half the helicopter's eight missiles at the Klar ship.

Four streaks of smoke like strings connected their helicopter and a huge explosion below. All four missiles seemed to hit the black monster as one.

Yet somehow it still seemed to be coming up and out.

McCallum could see damage on the Klar ship. Where once had been patterns of black and gray diamonds were scorch marks and dented hull. The missiles were clearly striking a hull, not some sort of force field.

The huge round Klar ship finally cleared the mouth of the cave and began to move upward, filling the canyon below it with a black shadow.

Four more missiles pounded it, knocking it back against the rocks.

It seemed to roll along the rock cliff face like a tire over a bumpy road. Then it lifted away slowly.

"Hit it with everything!" the general shouted.

Missiles streaked from the three choppers, including four more from theirs.

McCallum watched in amazement as the black ship lifted a short distance through the huge explosion.

It wasn't going to work.

They weren't going to be able to stop it.

Then the black hovering shape that floated over the desert like a big, dark rain cloud just seemed to come apart in the air.

A huge explosion of blue-and-white flame rolled out of the sky.

Then the big black ship simply ceased to be.

The shock wave from the explosion sent their chopper spinning backward and it took Ron a few long seconds to get it back under control. But he managed before they were pasted all over the rocks and sagebrush.

"Too close," Henry said.

McCallum was too busy trying to catch his breath to say anything in return.

As Ron stabilized the helicopter and turned it back toward the scene below, McCallum was amazed at the scene.

The desert was on fire.

Fire everywhere. Within a half mile, every stick, every sagebrush, every tree in the canyon, was burning with a bright orange flame, still too hot to even start sending smoke into the air.

Both the other helicopters had managed to stay up.

And there was absolutely no sign of the Klar ship.

Nothing but a burning desert.

And the wreckage of Red Bluff One.

43

Death is an incurable disease that men and women are born with; it gets them sooner or later.

—FREDRIC BROWN
FROM *THE SCREAMING MIMI*

4:32 P.M. JUNE 26.
SHEEPEATER CAVES, EASTERN OREGON

The roar overhead brought Tina up out of her nightmare.

The air in the cave felt as though it was pouring out of an oven, thick and hot, almost too hot to breathe. Her muscles ached and her head spun. As the roaring sound grew so that it filled the room, then passed beyond, she tried to sit up, but without luck. She was just too worn out, hungry, and thirsty to even move.

"What—" Cobb said beside her. But he didn't move either.

Around her nothing but the flies moved in the thick, dead air.

The rumbling seemed to hold steady for a short time.

Then an explosion shook the cave.

Dirt from above dropped onto her chest and arms and she somehow forced herself to sit up. Beside her, Cobb was working to push himself up on a rock.

Then everything went completely insane.

It was as if the entire earth was moving, exploding, shaking around her.

The ground seemed to heave under them, tossing her into the air and down hard on the dirt.

Cobb was tossed hard against the rock wall, and Tina watched as his eyes closed and he slumped to the ground.

Rocks smashed to the ground from above, opening the crack in the ceiling into an oblong hole of bright sunshine cutting through air filled with dust.

Again the ground and air seemed to explode around her.

She was flipped over backward and she could feel her right arm snap against a sharp boulder. The pain sent her head swirling, but somehow she was already so detached from her body that the broken arm didn't knock her out.

Another part of the ceiling came down, just missing her, but covering her in a thick layer of dirt and small pebbles. She quickly crawled over against the wall near Cobb.

Then the nightmare around her changed.

The room and time itself seemed to stand still as a bright blue-and-white flash lit every inch of the cave. She could see every body, every broken human, every rock in the cave.

And the heat increased.

Suddenly.

Intensely.

Two bodies right below the opening in the roof seemed to jerk, then their skin started to bubble and boil as if they were lying under a child's magnifying glass on a summer day.

Tina managed to drop behind a boulder as the smell of cooking human flesh filled the air.

Cobb moaned and before she passed out she managed to pull him down close to her under the shelter of the boulder.

44

No stupid man ever suspected himself of being anything but clever.

—THOMAS BAILEY ALDRICH
FROM *THE STILLWATER TRAGEDY*

4:41 P.M. JUNE 26.
SHEEPEATER CAVES, EASTERN OREGON

"Put us down," General Hoffman said to Ron. "In front of the cave. Red Bluff Two, take a position on top of the west wall overlooking the cave and scout that area. Red Bluff Three, stay in position above the east wall of the canyon. We're going to secure the cave."

The pilots moved like a well-oiled team, reacting to the general's orders.

McCallum managed to make himself take a deep breath of hot air as he studied the burning below him. The heat had been so intense from the alien craft's disintegration that almost everything combustible on the ground burst into flames instantly and was consumed within moments. Now thousands of small plumes of smoke drifted up into the hot air, forming a cloud of gray smoke that the blades of the helicopters stirred around as if they were stirring cream in hot tea.

There was no sign that an alien ship had ever been there. Nothing, not one little piece seemed to be left.

"You all right?" McCallum asked, forcing himself to turn away from the sight to look at Henry. His partner's face was pure white and he seemed to be panting slightly, but he nodded.

"Neda?" McCallum asked.

She turned away from the window to look at him. There was a light in her eyes. A bright light of excitement. "They're beatable," she said. "We've taken out one of their ships. I can't believe it happened. It did happen, didn't it?"

McCallum smiled. "Yeah, it happened."

Neda nodded to herself. "Good. One down and nineteen to go."

"I like the way she puts things," Henry said, shaking his head in disgust.

"Billy, get that door open and be ready," General Hoffman ordered.

"Yes, sir," the kid in front of McCallum said. He slid open the big side door on the chopper, pulled back the crank on the huge machine gun and swung it out the door. He quickly aimed it at the mouth of the cave below.

Ron was taking the helicopter down below the rim of the canyon. He was holding McCallum and Billy's side of the helicopter facing the huge opening, covering it with Billy's gun.

McCallum felt as though he was sitting in an open elevator dropping down into hell as the wind and heat swirled around him through the door. He could see the piles of rocks in the mouth of the cave, brought down by the explosions. The entire mouth of the cave looked as if someone had had a huge fire and blackened every rock with soot.

McCallum was sure that hell itself probably didn't look this bad, nor was it this hot.

"McCallum. Detective. Miss Foster," General Hoffman barked. "Get those belts and headphones off. Billy, arm them all. And get me one, too. We're going in, people. Miss Foster, since you're the farthest from the door I want you on the ground last and watching behind us. I want you following about twenty yards back to take out anything that pops up after we've gone past. Understand?"

"Yes, sir," she said.

McCallum unbuckled his seat belt and pulled off his headphones. The rumbling roar of the helicopter suddenly increased to a deafening, intense noise. Bobby handed him an AK-47 and an extra clip, then gave him the thumbs up.

McCallum made sure the gun was pointed out the side door of the chopper, then checked it. Loaded and ready to roll. He'd fired an AK-47 once at the police training range. The thing could spit out a stream of lead. And could hit what it was aimed at. One very nasty weapon in the wrong hands.

"Ready," Henry yelled over the sound of the motor, slapping his rifle.

Neda Foster gave a thumbs-up also.

McCallum answered with one of his own.

The helicopter set down with a hard bump in a blinding swirl of dirt, dust, and smoke that choked McCallum and filled his eyes with soot. How the hell was he supposed to see in this?

The general bailed out of the front door of the chopper and went right into the dust and smoke, up the slight incline toward the cave mouth.

McCallum moved almost at the same time and went to the left, stumbling in the blinding dust and smoke, but managing to keep the gun up in front of him and a clear picture of those Klar statues in his mind. If he saw one of those monsters coming at him through the dust he was going to shoot first and say hello later.

After ten yards the dust stirred by the helicopter blades cleared and the rest of the way to the mouth of the cave became clear.

McCallum could see Henry off his right shoulder, between him and the general. They all found shelter behind boulders near the mouth of the cave in the sun and paused.

McCallum could feel the intense heat radiating from the rock he was behind. And the entire place smelled a little like the room in Portland had smelled: death combined with melted plastic.

Henry touched the rock he was behind, then pulled his hand away as if he was burned.

This had to be the hottest place on the planet, without a doubt.

Neda took up a position about ten yards behind them, facing slightly back toward the chopper, but in such a way that she could see anything behind the men. McCallum felt secure with her in that position.

The general indicated they'd all go in together. He held up one finger, then two, then three as he jumped and went into the mouth of the cave at the best run he could manage over the rocks.

McCallum and Henry were both right beside him, picking their way like football players over and around the rocks while watching ahead. McCallum did his best to stay against the wall.

They were just inside the blackness of the cave when the

first shot cut through the air, a white light that hit a rock at McCallum's left and blew it apart as if a blasting cap had been placed inside it.

Pebbles stung his arm like a shotgun blast and he dove and rolled behind a nearby boulder. With only a slight stop he came up firing in the direction the light blast had come from.

Both Henry and the general were also firing, the mouth of the cave echoing with the sounds of three M-16s blasting and bullets ricocheting off rock inside.

McCallum stopped and made himself take a deep breath while his eyes adjusted to the darkness of the cave interior. He could tell the room was huge, with a high ceiling. The floor was mostly level, with a few scattered boulders that had obviously just fallen from the ceiling in the last battle. The shot had come from somewhere near the back of the cave.

Another white light from the same area blew apart a rock behind Henry.

McCallum couldn't see the target, but he had a good idea where it was now. He might be able to see it if he was farther down the left side of the cave in the rocks scattered there.

Henry had rolled to cover his head and the general was laying down return fire.

"Henry!" McCallum shouted.

Henry got up on one knee behind the boulder and gave a thumbs-up sign that he was all right.

McCallum pointed to himself and then down the left side of the cave.

Henry nodded. "Cover McCallum, General," Henry shouted.

Both of them at the same time sent bursts of fire into the area of the white light as McCallum jumped over a few rocks and ducked behind a large boulder on the left side of the cave. No alien shot at him, but one ricochet pinged against a rock right near his head.

After a long few seconds of sprinting, he was now ten paces farther inside, away from the mouth of the cave.

Now his eyes were adjusting to the blackness.

He could see two Klar tucked against the back wall of the cave, both with white stick-like things grasped in their hands. One of the Klar looked injured, and considering their cover and how many bullets were bouncing around them, it was amazing they were still alive.

McCallum's first instinct as a former cop was to shout "Surrender!" But he had no idea if they'd hear him and he didn't want to give away his position.

He dropped to the dirt and placed his M-16 on a small rock to steady the barrel. "This is war," he said softly to himself. These monsters had planned to blow up every human city on the planet. He owed them nothing.

One of the Klar rose up to aim his white stick in the direction of General Hoffman and Henry.

"This is for Albert Hancer, wherever he is," McCallum said, and pulled the trigger.

The stream of bullets cut through the Klar and spun the monster around, smashing him down into a rock.

The other one tried to get his white stick up in McCallum's direction, but McCallum covered him with a burst, sending him tumbling back on top of his buddy.

"Got them," McCallum shouted and both the general and Henry stopped firing.

Suddenly a white flash filled the cave, followed by a small thump.

Where the two Klar bodies had been was now a mass of smoking, steaming liquid. Like the thing-on-the-bed and their ship, they had simply disintegrated, leaving no real proof that they had existed.

45

No man is dead till he's dead.

—FRANCES BEEDING
FROM *THE TWELVE DISGUISES*

4:45 P.M. JUNE 26.
SHEEPEATER CAVES, EASTERN OREGON

Tina Harris came back to consciousness with the sound of firecrackers going off in the distance. For a short moment she thought she was back home over a hot Fourth of July. And she was missing all the fun.

Strings of firecrackers. What fun.

She so wanted to join the fun. She loved the Fourth and all the family things that went on.

Then she moved.

The pain from her broken arm shot through her dream and brought her upright. She could hardly breathe, the air was so thick and hot. The hole in the roof was five times its size before, and she could see smoke floating in the sky beyond the cave. And somewhere out there she could hear the sound of a motor.

Something had happened.

She eased over and tried to wake Cobb. He was still alive, but she didn't know for how long. He only groaned when she touched him.

She glanced around, holding her arm tight against her body. There was no one else in the room moving. Two human bodies lay blackened and smoking directly under the hole. A week ago the sight would have gagged her, but she had seen so much death now that it didn't. And somewhere in the back of her mind that fact bothered her.

A long burst of firecrackers in the distance.

Then silence.

Complete silence.

Those hadn't been firecrackers. Those had been gunshots.

She used her good arm to push herself to her feet and then stood in the intense heat, waiting for her head to stop spinning. After a moment it did.

She used the rocks in the room as things to lean on as she picked her way toward the door, moving around bodies. Every step jarred her broken arm, sending waves of pain up her shoulder and into her neck. She doubted if she could get back across the small cave to Cobb. But if there was help coming out there, someone had to let them know there were people in here. And she was the only one still moving, from what she could tell.

She reached the metal barrier, the door the aliens had constructed in the mouth of the cave. It looked as if it was crafted out of parts of a rusted old car.

She tried hitting it with her fist, but the blow sent shock waves of pain through her, making her lose her breath. And the sound she made wouldn't attract anything.

She stepped back, picked up a small rock and moved to the metal barrier, where she sat down on the ground. Then, slowly, she began tapping the rock on the metal

Slowly and as consistently as she could.

Tap. Tap. Tap.

On and on.

The sound seemed to echo in the small room. And from somewhere there was a moan.

But otherwise she was alone, tapping the rock on the metal, giving her last strength to a hope of rescue.

46

Test an absurdity and you may stumble on a truth.

—ROY C. VICKERS
FROM *THE DEPARTMENT OF DEAD ENDS*

4:52 P.M. JUNE 26.
SHEEPEATER CAVES, EASTERN OREGON

The large cave seemed to deaden every sound as McCallum, Henry, Neda Foster, and General Hoffman scoured it for any sign of aliens. It took only a few minutes for them to call the cave secure.

Outside, the two helicopters standing guard landed and shut down. This fight was over.

But McCallum knew the war had just begun.

The aliens had left only two of their crew, most likely because they didn't have time to get back aboard. And now those two were nothing more than a puddle of stinking acid, slowly soaking into the ground.

McCallum sat on a rock near the remains of the two Klar, doing his best to catch his breath. His M-16 leaned against his leg, giving him a sense of security in the half-light. Even with the darker insides of the cave, the temperature had to be well over a hundred degrees. Henry stood near him, staring at the puddle of acid, his rifle slung over his shoulder. It was as if neither of them wanted to be far from their weapons.

Neda Foster and the general had gone back to the helicopter to report to the president. General Hoffman said he was going to bring in a crew and secure the area, calling it a crash site. Red Bluff One had crashed on a training exercise and he was going to make sure all his men had the same story down pat.

Another government cover-up, and this time McCallum was square in the middle of it. Amazing the positions a man minding his own business finds himself in.

"I'm going to stand under a cold shower for an hour when we get back," Henry said. "Just to see if I can remember what being cold feels like."

"Sounds wonderful," McCallum agreed. "But I think I'll start with a full pitcher of iced tea." Sweat was pouring off him and he was starting to get a little dizzy. He knew that both he and Henry needed water soon.

"Yeah," Henry said. "And after that a—"

Henry suddenly stopped talking and McCallum sprang to his feet, gun in hand, as a faint tapping echoed through the cave. They both strained to listen. McCallum couldn't tell where it was coming from, but it sounded weak and distant. But it was clearly from inside the cave, even though he thought they had checked every part of the place.

"What is that?" Henry said.

"Maybe," McCallum said, "we have some abductees in here somewhere."

"Shit!" Henry said. "You may be right. I'll yell for some

flashlights." At a fast run he started back toward the mouth of the cave.

"Have them bring water and medical supplies, too," McCallum shouted after him.

Henry raised his arm to show that he heard without breaking stride.

McCallum moved slowly toward the back of the large chamber, trying to follow the tapping. Near the back were a few small indents in the rock wall, but all of them were dead ends. Or at least he thought they were. He checked each one as best as he could without light, finding nothing. But the tapping continued, faintly.

He didn't seem to be getting any closer.

"Keep it up," he said softly. "We'll find you."

Henry, Neda, and the general came scrambling at full clip into the mouth of the cave, switching on flashlight beams as they came. The lights added some depth to the cave, but not much.

And they reminded McCallum of the Klar weapon, but not enough to want the lights turned off.

"Any luck?" Henry shouted halfway across the floor.

"Nothing," McCallum said. "But I have an idea. Everyone spread out to different parts of the cave and stand still. Then point in the direction you think the sound is coming from. We'll see if we can get some triangulation on this."

The three scattered, taking up positions around the large cavern. Then they stopped and listened.

McCallum thought the tapping came from the back of the cave to the right, but there wasn't anything back there that he could see except stone wall. He still pointed in that direction.

Henry pointed near where the aliens had died, also to the right.

Neda and the general did the same.

"Okay," McCallum said, heading for the back right wall. With flashlights it only took him a moment to see where the tapping was coming from. There used to be a small corridor leading off the big room, but rocks had come down, probably during the attack, and blocked it. The tapping was coming from behind those rocks.

"Hello!" McCallum shouted at the rock slide. "Anyone there?"

The tapping stopped and McCallum could hear a faint, "Yes. We're here."

"Help is on the way," McCallum shouted.

There were two taps and then silence.

McCallum looked at the pile of rock filling the corridor, then turned to the general. "Sir, we need young, strong help here."

"You got it," the general said. He turned and at a fast trot headed back toward the mouth of the cave.

"You got some water?" McCallum asked and Henry tossed him a canteen.

McCallum took a full drink, savoring the feel of the warm liquid as it washed the dirt and dryness out of his mouth. He tossed it back to Henry. "Both of you do the same thing."

"Gladly," Henry said, tipping up the canteen, then passing it to Neda.

McCallum turned and climbed as high as he could on the rock slide filling the narrow corridor. Then slowly he pulled down the first rock and passed it to Henry.

Five minutes later the young army pilots and gunners took over as Neda, Henry, and McCallum stepped back, sweating.

Another ten minutes and they had uncovered a metal wall made out of rusted old car bodies.

Neda studied it from behind where the young guys were working, clearing the last of the rocks. "The Klar are so careful," she said. "They didn't even use their own stuff to build a prison. They did the same in the mine where I was held."

There was no lock on the door, just a large board to stop the door from opening. McCallum and Henry moved in to open the door, and McCallum swung it open.

And in front of him was a sight that would give him nightmares for years.

The smell of burnt human flesh and rotting bodies smashed into him, making him stagger back. Behind him McCallum could hear one of the young army pilots throwing up.

"Oh, my God," Henry said.

Thirty naked bodies were scattered around the small cave. Over half of them had clearly been dead for days. All the bodies were covered with dirt and flies.

This room must have been like an oven every day. And then the Klar ship's explosion must have sent intense heat straight down in here. In the center of the room, directly under a hole, were two bodies charred into blackness.

Beside the door a thin, dirt-covered naked woman leaned against the wall. She held a clearly broken right arm with her left hand. She was looking up at him, smiling, her white teeth the only thing clean on her.

Both Henry and McCallum knelt down beside her.

She smiled at both of them, then said, her voice hoarse, "Dr. Livingston, I presume?"

"More like Laurel and Hardy," McCallum said after a moment of shock.

She laughed, then grimaced as the pain from her arm shot through her.

"You stay still and we'll get you out of here."

"Oh, heaven help us," the general said, stepping through the door, covering his nose.

McCallum watched as the general took one slow look around. Then he said, low and angrily, "Those alien bastards."

"He's got that one right," the woman on the floor said, and Henry laughed.

The general glanced at the hole in the roof then turned to his men who were standing, mouths open in shock, staring through the door. Quickly he started barking orders. "Two of you go find that hole up there from the outside. Then rig up some sort of pulley so that we can get the wounded through there to be airlifted out."

The two in the back turned and ran.

"Ron," General Hoffman continued snapping orders. "I want you to call Gowen Field in Boise and tell General Prior that I'm calling in a favor. I want him to set up a secure medical hospital and be prepared for wounded. Only a few trusted doctors and nurses, no one else. Understand?"

"Yes, sir," Ron said. "I'll make it clear to him."

"The rest of you find any medical supplies and water in those choppers you can get and return here. Move!"

His men responded as though someone was shooting at them. As a unit the rest of them turned and at a full run headed toward the cave mouth.

McCallum and Henry were still kneeling beside the young woman. "Can you check on the blond guy near the back of the cave?" she asked. "He was hurt bad in that last explosion."

"I'll do it," Henry said.

Neda Foster was already working her way into the cave, checking to see who was still alive. As McCallum and the young girl watched, Henry moved the length of the room and knelt over a body against the far wall. After a moment he looked up, smiling. "He's alive."

"Great," the woman said, seeming to relax back against the stone wall with the news.

"I'm McCallum," he said. Then he pointed at Neda. "That's Neda Foster from Bellingham, Washington. And the fat guy who checked out your friend is Detective Henry Greer from Portland."

"Tina," the woman said.

"Tina Harris?" McCallum asked.

"You're kidding," Henry said as he again knelt down beside her. "You're Tina Harris?"

The woman looked up at McCallum. "I see my dad's been looking for me."

McCallum laughed. "He hired me to find you."

"Well," Tina said, smiling up at McCallum. "I'm very glad you're a good detective."

"Not that good," McCallum said. "Just the world's luckiest."

"Is there a difference?" Tina asked.

McCallum thought Henry was never going to stop laughing.

47

Heaven pity the person who tries to tell all the truth.

—JOHN DICKSON CARR
FROM *THE CROOKED HINGE*

8:38 P.M. JUNE 26.
WASHINGTON, D.C.

Vice President Alan Wallace dropped the folder on the desk of the president, glad to be rid of it. "There were nine survivors, sir. All have been airlifted to a secured hospital ward at Gowen Field Air Base in Boise."

"Good," the president said, standing and moving around the desk. He indicated that the vice president should sit on the couch, then sat down in a chair across from him. There were a crystal decanter of brandy and two glasses on the coffee table between them.

John picked up the brandy and began to pour while talking. "What about the crash site?"

"Secured," Alan said, getting himself as comfortable as

he could. "And the chopper crew's families have been notified."

"What about the dead in the cave?"

"We're going to take that slow," Alan said. "Most likely we'll have each body turn up near where the person was abducted." That decision had been the hardest for Alan to make, but he didn't mention that to John. At least, eventually, the families would have closure. Better than most of those abducted by the Klar.

The president nodded sadly. He finished pouring both glasses, and put the brandy down. "Has General Hoffman got his people ready for tomorrow?"

"He does, sir," Alan said. "They'll be heading for Texas tonight for staging. They'll see if they can surprise the Klar in Mexico tomorrow morning. We've got four more attack helicopters added to his command and he'll brief the crews."

"And my offer?" the president asked.

"He accepted it with honor, he said, sir. He wants the base for the special task force to be in the Seattle area."

"To be near Foster's organization," John said. "Smart man, General Hoffman."

"Actually, sir," Alan said, "I think he just likes it there."

John laughed, then got very serious. "So how do we stand, Alan? Are we going to see tomorrow morning?"

Alan smiled. "The Foster organization thinks that finding all the bombs and destroying one of the ships has set the Klar invasion plans back years. The Klar are so careful and conservative that it will take them a long time to come up with another attack plan they will dare to use."

"And Foster's people, along with General Hoffman, will keep them on the run in the meantime."

"That's the idea, sir," Alan said. "Maybe even find a way to stop them for good."

John picked up a glass of brandy and handed it to Alan. It felt cool in his hands.

"For the first time in days, I think that's something we can drink to," the president said, picking up his glass and holding it out. Then, before he took a drink, he got very serious. "Nice job, Alan. I can't thank you publicly, but I can thank you here, for the people of the country."

He saluted the vice president with his glass.

Alan raised his glass in acknowledgment. "I think they'd owe you a thanks, too," Alan said, saluting his president.

"We did win the first one," John said, smiling.

"That we did," Alan said, smiling in return.

Then both of them drank.

And it tasted wonderful to Alan, that flavor of victory.

Epilogue

It would be the height of idiocy to deny oneself wine merely to live a little longer.

—ROBERT BARNARD
FROM *UNRULY SON*

8:10 P.M. JULY 8.
PORTLAND, OREGON

McCallum pushed himself back slightly from the table and tossed his cloth napkin on his empty plate. He felt full and very satisfied after one of the largest steaks he'd had in years.

Mr. and Mrs. Harris, with their daughter Tina, sat around the end of the cloth-covered table in Bristol's, one of Portland's finest restaurants. Tina's arm was still in a sling, but otherwise she looked healthy. McCallum could still see deep shadows under her eyes. He doubted those shadows would ever leave her.

Next to the Harrises on the left side of the table were Neda Foster, her father, and Dr. Cornell. They had flown down from Seattle especially for this dinner.

McCallum sat at the foot of the table facing Mr. Harris, with Claudia to his right, Henry to her right, and Mayor Osborne next to Mrs. Harris. They were all dressed up in their best evening wear. McCallum had on his best suit and had actually whistled at Claudia when he saw her. She was simply stunning in a long, gold evening dress. No other words for it.

Mr. Harris had reserved a private room tucked in the back of the restaurant. A room full of food, wine, and service that only money like Mr. Harris's could buy. It had been a wonderful dinner so far.

In the twelve days since the fight in the Sheepeater Caves, Neda's group, using McCallum's string method, had pinpointed eight possible locations of Klar ships. General Hoffman and his helicopter troops had destroyed two more Klar ships and sent the others they spotted packing into space, dented.

The press was still hounding the mayor about the "unexplained explosions," but no new leads were developing and there was always more news. And the article about the helicopter crash in eastern Oregon had made the third page of the paper and nothing more.

There were no signs of Albert Hancer or Tina's boyfriend, Jerry Rodale. Tina had gone to visit his parents with her father, and McCallum had no idea what she told them. The young student named Cobb, who dug the tunnel with her, lived, but was still in the hospital in Boise.

After the first night in Boise, McCallum had gone back to his office and had somehow managed over the last twelve days to get things in order and moving slowly forward. But he still hadn't repaired the bullet holes that Evan had put in his office wall. He was starting to agree with Henry that they added something to the office. He had also managed to read eight new detective novels, none of which he'd liked enough to put on the special bookshelf in his office.

"So," Henry said, looking around, "where's the dessert tray?"

Around the table, others laughed and McCallum said, "They'll bring it around when everyone's finished, you dolt."

Mr. Harris tossed his napkin on his plate and stood, smiling. "Maybe now, *before* dessert, would be a good time to give our announcement?"

He glanced at Tina and she nodded yes.

Mr. Harris faced the table. "I've thanked each and every one of you personally for finding Tina. And I want to do that one more time right now." He took a deep breath. "Thank you. One and all."

McCallum could tell it was thanks from the heart.

"Yes, thank you all," Tina chimed in.

There was a moment of uneasy silence as everyone smiled. McCallum was actually impressed that Henry didn't chime in with a smart remark.

"Tina has asked a favor of me," Mr. Harris said after a long moment of silence. "She asked me to allow her to drop out of college for the time being."

"You're sure, Tina?" Claudia asked. "College is important."

"Yeah," Henry said, "you might end up like me if you don't go."

"You have a college degree," McCallum said.

"Just trying to help," Henry said, and everyone laughed.

"Don't worry," Tina said. "I've promised that I will return when the time is right."

"She has also asked me for another favor," Mr. Harris said, smiling. "She's asked me to fund an organization like the Fosters' organization in Seattle, only based here in Portland. A second group focused on stopping the Klar. I've agree on two conditions."

"Wonderful," Neda Foster said, clapping. "Simply wonderful."

McCallum was shocked, but pleased. The more money behind the search for a way to stop the Klar, the better off they would all be in the long run.

"I'm glad, Neda, that you think so," Tina said, smiling a huge smile. "Because one of Father's conditions is that we work closely with your group and General Hoffman. Sort of a side branch down here. Would that be all right?"

"All right?" Neda said, laughing. "Better than all right. More like *wonderful*."

"Great," Tina said.

"So what's condition two?" Henry asked.

Mr. Harris stared down the table at McCallum. McCallum knew something was coming, but he was like a deer caught in the headlights of a car. There was just no place to run.

"The second condition," Mr. Harris said, "is that Richard McCallum work for the organization."

Tina had a worried look on her face, staring down the table at him.

McCallum was totally caught by surprise. "I have a going investigation business," McCallum said.

"I know," Mr. Harris said, still smiling. "I want to hire you and your firm to work with Tina and her organization. Full time or part time, your choice as you see fit. But I want you on board."

McCallum glanced at Claudia, who was smiling, then at Henry, who was also smiling and nodding yes.

McCallum turned back to Tina Harris. "You sure you

want to work with me? I can be a real opinionated pain."

"He's noticed," Henry said. "I'm shocked."

Tina laughed. "More than sure, Mr. McCallum. I feel we need you to give us all a real fighting chance."

McCallum took a deep breath. He had been wondering what he was going to do in the coming fights against the Klar. It had felt a little odd to him to just go back to being an investigator without being involved somewhere. Now, here was his chance.

"Okay," he said. "I'd be honored and pleased to be on board. Thanks for the offer."

With that everyone cheered.

And a half-dozen toasts later Henry finally got dessert.